Title: Speed of light

Lexile: 540
Reading Lvl: n/a

DATE DUE

DEC 19 06			
DEC 3 07			
DEC 3 07			
MAR 1 8 2008			
JAN 24 '14			
DEC 1 9 2014			

speed of light

by sybil rosen

An Anne Schwartz Book

ATHENEUM BOOKS FOR YOUNG READERS

For my parents,
Sam and Jeannette Rosen,
and
to the memory of
Michael Topiol

Atheneum Books for Young Readers
An imprint of Simon & Schuster Children's Publishing Division
1230 Avenue of the Americas
New York, New York 10020
Book design by Ann Bobco
The text of this book is set in Century Schoolbook.
Printed in the United States of America
10 9 8 7 6 5 4
Library of Congress Cataloging-in-Publication Data
Rosen, Sybil.
Speed of light / by Sybil Rosen.—1st ed.
"An Anne Schwartz book."
Summary: An eleven-year-old Jewish girl living in the South during the
1950s struggles with the anti-Semitism and racism which pervade her small
community.
ISBN 0-689-82437-8
[1. Anti-semitism—Fiction. 2. Racism—Fiction. 3. Jews—United States—
Fiction. 4. Prejudices—Fiction.] I. Title.
PZ7.R718715Sp 1999
[Fic]—dc21
98-40546

Acknowledgments

I want to thank the people who so generously fed the writing of this book: Eugenie and Julien Sacks, Rabbi Jerome Fox, Adam Scher, Reverend Carl Hutcherson, Jr., Robert Treuhaft, Konrad Ryushin Marchaj, Betty Boomer, Mary Pope Osborne, Michael Yukon Grody, Craig and Amelia Penland Fuller, Katherine Cortez, Marnie Andrews, Pril Smiley, Janet Swords, June Stein, Ann Walton, Sarah Chodoff, Casey Kurtti, Chuck and Judy Perrenod, Louis Ravina, Frank Cuttita, Betsy Cornwall, Greg Burns, Reba Laks, Kathy Ambrosini, Patricia Murphy, Barbara Altomare, Robi Josephson, Ilka List, David Cree, Susan Castner, Josh and Karen Rosen, Pauline Berson, and especially my agent, Richard Basch, for his loyalty and good humor. A heartfelt thanks also goes to Judy Krueger, principal of St. Mary of the Lake School in New Buffalo, Michigan, and members of Ruta Augustaitis's sixth-grade class — Julie Baughman, Randy Deaton, Anna de Caneva, Alicia Merchant, Melanie Oudhuis, Michael Pawlik, Alisa Rahm, Jacob Shreve, Eric Umbrasas — for their attention, insight, and creativity. And to my editor, Anne Schwartz, I offer my deep gratitude; without her honesty, patience, and unshakable faith, Audrey's story would not have come alive.

1

The day before my face broke out in the shape of the Big Dipper, a rock came flying through a window of my daddy's pajama factory. Slivers of glass shot across the room, shattering the hush of a hot, sleepy Virginia afternoon. It was the third of June; fifth grade had ended that same Friday.

Daddy told us all about it at supper that night. "It came out of nowhere" was how he described it. A frown made his black brows dip down over his nose.

"Ooh," I breathed. In my mind's eye I could see those tiny shards sparkling in the sunlight before going every which way.

My mother's voice banished my daydream. "Audrey Ina, quit oohing and pass your daddy the *kasha*, please, ma'am."

The kasha was a treat Tante Pesel had made. My aunt had inspected every grain of the coarse buckwheat before soaking them in vinegar; then she'd minced onions and garlic with her quick fingers to add to the mixture. Polish by birth, Tante sometimes cooked for us the unusual foods she'd eaten as a child.

"Mmm," Momma crooned as I swung the bowl toward Daddy. "Tante, it smells divine."

My aunt's eyes shimmered briefly, huge in her heart-shaped face. They were gray as rain, ringed in long lashes, drooping at the corners as if weighted down.

"What happened next, Daddy?" I asked, eager to learn more about that window.

"The rock knocked the head off a mannequin and rolled to a stop," he answered, deadpan.

Now my brother, Joel, grabbed the salt shaker and conked himself on the head with it, falling back, tongue lolling out. At four years old, Brother had electric blue eyes and a gap in his grin where a front tooth had broke off.

Momma removed the shaker from his hand. "Behave yourself, *noodnik*, you're at table now." An amused look passed between her and my aunt. "Tante, honey, help Brother to the kasha, would you, please?"

"Yucky," Joel declared. "Looks like termites."

"You promise me you try it," Tante coaxed in her curious accent. "Come, it will make you strong."

"Strong like bull?" Brother could imitate her to a T.

"No, strong like flea," she answered, making Joel shout with laughter and cram kasha into his mouth.

Momma rolled her eyes. "Joel, chew with your mouth closed, please, and keep still. I want to hear more about the factory." Her forehead creased. "Nathan, it's a mercy no one was hurt."

"No one living, you mean, Momma," I cracked.

"Oh, true," she replied. "Let us not forget that poor dummy. What time of day was it, anyhow?" she asked Daddy.

"About three, I'd say."

"Anybody see who threw it?" I asked.

"That's the thing of it," my father answered. "I went down on the avenue to ask. Nobody that I spoke to saw anything."

2

"That's strange," I remarked. "I mean, Campbell Avenue's mighty busy on a Friday afternoon. You'd think somebody saw something."

"You would think." My father picked kasha out of his teeth. "It surprised me too."

"Why should it surprise you?" Something harsh in Tante's tone made me look up at her. Her face seemed older than its twenty-four years, pale beneath a cap of colorless hair. Two small flames danced on her shoulder. The lights burned from candles on the countertop behind her, but from where I sat, they looked like they were rising from the black silk of her dress.

Friday evening was the start of the Jewish Sabbath, so Momma had lit the Shabbos candles and said the Hebrew blessing before sitting down to eat. The flames flickered like stars, like broken pieces of glass. All at once I saw that rock hurling down from outer space, crashing through the window of Stern's Nightwear and Company—

"I know!" I exclaimed.

Momma put a hand to her heart. "Honestly, Audrey Ina, you like to make me faint."

"Sorry, Momma, but I was just thinking, maybe it was a meteorite."

She blinked. "Come again?"

"That rock, I mean."

Tante fixed her great cold eyes on me. "And what makes you think this rock is meteorite?"

"Well, wouldn't that explain why nobody saw who threw it?"

Daddy chuckled. "You have to admit it's an interesting theory."

My aunt leaned toward Joel. "Pay no attention to your sister," she whispered. "We all know she is a little *meshugge*."

That stung. Meshugge was a Yiddish word, a language the grown-ups used to talk in secret among themselves. Joel twirled three circles beside his ear and pointed to me; even he knew meshugge meant "crazy in the head."

"Shut up, dummy," I barked at him. "I'll knock your block off for real."

"Audrey Ina," my mother cautioned. She turned to my aunt. "Tante, please, I've asked you not to tease Audrey like that."

"How can I help it?" she returned. "When she is talking always nonsense."

"It is *not* nonsense," I shot back.

"Now quit." Momma blew damp bangs off her forehead. "Honestly, the two of you are peas in a pod."

I pushed some kasha around my plate, frowning. I wasn't any more like Tante than Momma was. Why, if my mother was the sun, my aunt was the moon, shadowy and changeable.

Now Tante scowled at my father. "I am telling you, Nathan, this window is the beginning. Did you forget already Kristallnacht?"

I didn't know what Kristallnacht was, but I guessed from how she said it that it had to do with the war—World War II, that is. My aunt had spent that entire war in Poland, a prisoner of Adolf Hitler and the German Nazis. And even though this was 1956—and Hitler had been defeated eleven years ago—my father often said the war was still not over for Tante.

"I didn't forget anything," he told her now. "But this is not Poland, Tante. You're in America, remember?"

"America," she scoffed. "People are the same everywhere. They hated us there, they can hate us here. How is it different?"

Now I knew what she was on about. Seemed like anytime anything happened, no matter how small—if someone so much as looked at us funny—Tante was convinced they were anti-Semitic, prejudiced against Jews. True, there were a few like that in Blue Gap, but not everybody was, despite what my aunt thought.

Momma cleared her throat. "Tante, *das kindt*." Kindt meant "child." She turned to Joel. "Brother, you may be excused."

"Yippee!" He scrambled off his chair. "What's for dessert?"

"A slice of watermelon to eat on the porch, how's that?"

Joel grinned. "And will you come spit seeds with me, Daddy?"

My father glanced at his watch. "Not tonight, son. I have to go out."

Brother's face fell. "Again?"

Used to be my father played with Joel and me every evening. Only all this spring he'd been too busy for us, going out after supper and staying away long after we were in bed.

Brother fidgeted in the doorway till Tante took pity on him. "Go on, noodnik," she said. "I will come out with you in a minute."

Momma handed him the dripping melon. "Now scoot."

Soon as the screen door banged shut behind Joel, I turned to my aunt. "Tante, you don't really think that window got broke because Daddy's Jewish, do you?"

She threw up her hands. "Yes, genius, I do."

"Tante." Momma's voice was sharp. "She's eleven, you know? She's a child, she's just asking." She sat down. "I think you should tell her, Nat."

"Tell me what?" I asked.

Daddy took Momma's hand. "That's why I brought it up in the first place, Selma."

His eyes traveled from Tante to me. "I know I've been gone a lot lately. Truth is, I've been spending time with Mr. Cardwell. Y'all know him."

"Of course, Daddy." Mr. Cardwell worked as the watchman at Stern's Nightwear. Some folks might call him colored, but my daddy had taught us to say Negro, out of respect.

My father said, "Well, this morning Mr. Cardwell applied for a new job. A different job, not at the factory."

"Why?" I asked. "Are you firing him?"

Daddy smiled. "Not hardly. I went with him to apply."

"Then what's he want a new job for, anyway?"

"Let's just say he's hoping for a little more responsibility than what he has now," my father hedged.

"Like what?" It was common knowledge there weren't many jobs in Blue Gap Negroes could get. They could work as janitors or cooks or housekeepers, that was about it.

Daddy cleared his throat. "Like being a policeman."

The back of my neck prickled. A Negro policeman in Blue Gap? I'd never heard of such a thing. Far as I knew, most everybody in town was racist, prejudiced against Negroes. "Can he do that?" I wondered out loud.

"He's going to try," my father replied. "The police department is looking to hire a new officer." He slid his eyes to my aunt. "And I'm going to do what I can to help him get the job."

Tante snorted and lit a cigarette; apparently she already knew about this.

Now it hit me. "Oh, so you think that's why the window got broke? On account of Mr. Cardwell?"

"It's possible," my daddy allowed. "If someone got wind of what he's up to, they may have wanted to send him a warning."

"And not only to Mr. Cardwell, Nathan," Tante said. "That window is a warning to you also."

I turned to Daddy. "Is that so?"

"It could be," he answered. "Folks might not appreciate me trying to help him."

I thought a moment. "Then do you think there'll be more trouble?"

"Tell you what, Audrey. Let's not worry about that yet, okay?"

I shrugged. "Okay."

He cupped a hand under my chin. "That's my good girl."

Tante rose now, straight and tall. "Do not worry, he says. For me, it would be easier to fly to the moon." And she turned on her heel and went out.

Daddy followed her with his eyes. "I mean it, Audrey Ina. I really do believe this will work out in the end."

"If you say so, Daddy," I said.

*　　*　　*

Right after supper my folks went up to their bedroom and closed the door. Most Friday evenings we all got dressed in our Shabbos finery and drove to services at the synagogue downtown. But during dessert my mother announced that tonight she and Daddy were going to a town council meeting instead. My father had sat on the Blue Gap Town Council for two years now, the first Jewish man ever to be elected to it.

"Tonight?" I was surprised. Town council meetings were usually held the last Wednesday of each month.

"I've called a special meeting," my father explained. "To talk about Mr. Cardwell joining the police force."

"Oh," I said. "So can I go too?"

My mother smiled. "I don't think so."

"Why not, Momma? I'm curious to hear what folks have to say about this." I turned to my father. "Can I, please?"

"No, Audrey." Then Daddy and Momma got up, leaving me with the dishes.

From the kitchen sink I could see out the window that faced to the west. Blue Gap was a mill town in the Blue Ridge Mountains of Virginia. Smokestacks from the paper mills poked up over the rooftops, and behind them a wave of worn mountains curved against the sky. Feathery clouds faded from pink to gray in the long June twilight.

The smell of wild onion came in on the breeze; blossom-laden mimosas swayed in the front yard. Today had been the last day of the school year. For weeks I'd been dreaming of lazy bike rides through town, sunlit swims at the creek, shooting stars and fireflies at night.

Only suddenly summer seemed very far away. My father had told me not to worry, but something gnawed at me anyhow. If folks were mad enough about Mr. Cardwell to break a window, what else might they do?

I heard Tante come in through the cellar door and go into her room. Before Joel was born, her bedroom had been upstairs, like the rest of ours. But with only three bedrooms, Joel's crib had gone into hers, and Daddy had fixed up a room for her in the basement, where she could have more privacy. Now she clicked on the radio. Every evening she listened to Radio Free Europe, broadcasting in Polish. The foreign voices floated up the stairs.

I didn't know all that much about Tante, really. First off, she was not actually my aunt; she was a distant cousin of my mother's. But we all called her Tante, the Yiddish word for aunt, out of respect—even my parents who were older than her. My father said when someone has suffered a great deal, they earn your respect.

Tante's mother and Momma's mother—my grandma Lena—were second cousins. As children they'd played together in a country village in Poland, a village so small, Grandma sometimes joked, it didn't have a name. In fact, its name was Jarzyna, which was pronounced Yarzina; it meant "vegetable." Forty years ago Grandma Lena's family had left Jarzyna and eventually settled in Charlottesville, a hundred miles east of Blue Gap. Tante's family had stayed in Poland, and that was how Tante happened to be born there.

When World War II broke out, Tante's entire family— her father, mother, and older sister Gitel—were killed by the Nazis. She herself had spent two years in a kind of prison called a concentration camp, someplace named Auschwitz. That was really all my parents had told me about her. And Tante rarely talked about her life—not to me anyhow.

I was wiping down the counters when I heard her come up the stairs. My heart began to knock the way it did sometimes when my aunt approached me. A tray of dishes rattled in her hands.

"You okay, Tante?" I asked politelike.

Without a word she slid the tray toward me. Glasses were brown with coffee stains, dried tea bags stuck to cups, saucers brimmed with cigarette stubs. It would take me twenty minutes to scrub everything clean.

But I smiled with my lips and said, "Thank you, Tante," just as my father would have wanted. Her eyes passed through me like I was not even there. In the little gust caused by her leaving, ashes blew on the clean countertop.

I listened to her footsteps fall away on the stairs. Tante was thirteen years old when she'd come here to live with us after the war; I'd been only three months old. So many times I'd wondered what our house would be like without her dark cloud hovering above it.

I'd just finished putting Tante's dishes away when my folks came down, dressed for the meeting. Momma bent to kiss me good-bye.

"Tante'll put Brother to bed," she told me. "You can stay up, but don't forget, we're going to services bright and early in the morning."

I wiped my hands on my shorts. "Can't I go with you? Please. Come on, I'll be good. I won't say a word."

"Audrey, now no—" my mother began.

"But, Momma, I'm dying to see if there's anyone in Blue Gap who'd even want Mr. Cardwell as a policeman. I just can't imagine it. On Mars maybe, but not here."

My daddy took my hands. "Audrey, of course there are other people in town who want Mr. Cardwell to get the job."

"And will they be at the meeting too?" I asked.

"Yes." He glanced at the kitchen clock. "I'll tell you all about it in the morning, okay?"

I folded my arms, sulking, as they went out the back door. Hearing them linger on the patio, I crept to the window to listen.

My father was saying, "You know, Selma, maybe it's not such a bad idea for her to come with us. She needs to see for herself what we're up against here. She's old enough to handle it."

"But, Nathan," Momma said back, "you have no idea what might happen at this meeting. What if there's trouble?"

"As long as you and I are with her, she'll be all right."

I heard my mother sigh. Daddy called back, "Audrey Ina? Is that you at the window?"

I gulped. "Yes, sir."

"Wash your face and come on," he said.

2

A handful of stars were winking over the courthouse when we arrived. The meeting was being held in a small room off the main courtroom and its thirty chairs had already started to fill.

"How'd folks find out about this so fast?" I asked Momma.

"I thought you weren't going to say a word." She cut her eyes at me. "You know how Blue Gap is, Audrey. News travels like wildfire."

She pointed me to a seat near the back. "Sit there and don't move a muscle." Then she turned to say hello to Mr. Cardwell, his wife, Frances, who was also our housekeeper, and their twelve-year-old son, Sam. They were all standing at the back of the room.

I was amazed; I'd never heard of Negroes attending a town council meeting before. Only Sam looked as surprised to see me there as I was to see him. We knew each other some; he took care of our yard to make extra money. He threw me a quick wave and I returned it.

Behind him stood Reverend Owen Hutcherson and several other members of the Cardwells' church. In front of me, white folks were settling into metal folding chairs. Most threw shocked glances at the Negroes gathered in back. Still, I noticed there were other white people besides

Momma and me seated near the Cardwells and their friends.

Now the five men on council, Daddy among them, took their seats at a table in front. The council president was a dour man named Mr. Pearson. He rapped on the table with his fist.

The second the chatter died down, someone yelled out, "Who said they could come?" and jerked a thumb toward the Negroes at the back.

Mr. Pearson frowned. "I believe I'll let Mr. Stern answer that question."

Somebody hissed. I craned my neck to see who it was, but Momma put a hand on my arm and shook her head.

Daddy stood, clearing his throat. "I thought that since this meeting was called to discuss the possibility of Lovelle Cardwell becoming a policeman here in Blue Gap, it was only fair that he and his supporters attend."

A grumble began to spread through the room. "I realize the prospect of a Negro cop is not a popular one," my father kept on.

"You got that right," another man shouted.

Mr. Pearson struck the table. "This will be an orderly meeting, no matter what," he declared. "Anyone talking out of turn will be asked to leave."

My daddy continued. "I called this meeting to ask town council to vote in support of Mr. Cardwell's efforts to join our police force."

The councilmen cast uncomfortable glances at one another. The grumble grew louder.

A councilman spoke up. "Mr. Stern, with all due respect, it's not up to council to decide whether Cardwell gets hired. That honor," he drawled, "belongs to Police Chief Monroe."

Every head swiveled toward the police chief. He leaned against a wall, arms across his chest. Elmo Monroe was a big, gruff man with a permanent piece of chewing tobacco pooching out his cheek.

"Mr. Monroe, would you care to comment?" Mr. Pearson asked.

The police chief worried the lump in his cheek. "I would not."

"We're counting on you, Elmo," a woman called.

Mr. Pearson slapped the table for quiet. The same councilman kept on. "That being the case, Mr. Stern, I can't see that it matters whether council supports Cardwell or not."

"Of course it matters," my father returned. "If council is behind Mr. Cardwell, it'll send a message to the citizens of Blue Gap. It might encourage others to come out for him too. And if enough folks express their approval, maybe that'll make Mr. Monroe's decision easier."

The grumble filled the room. Mr. Pearson struck the table. A lady with a blond beehive hairdo raised a gloved hand. Mr. Pearson nodded at her.

"Mr. Stern." She spoke to my daddy in a haughty manner. "What you are proposing is, quite simply, preposterous. If a colored man wants to better himself, surely he can try. Heaven knows you people have done well enough here."

"What people does she mean, Momma?" I whispered.

"She means us, Audrey," my mother replied, tight-lipped. "Us Jews."

The lady went on. "But a police officer, Mr. Stern? An officer must be someone who commands our respect. You can't seriously entertain that the people of Blue Gap could give a colored man the necessary respect."

"Why not?" my father returned.

I glanced back at Sam and the Cardwells. They stood listening, somber expressions on their faces.

Daddy addressed the entire room. "I think we all need to realize something. Like it or not, two years ago the Supreme Court ruled it unconstitutional for white children and Negro children to attend separate, segregated schools. Yet not a single step has been taken in Blue Gap to integrate our schools. Or anything else in our community."

I heard a woman whisper, "I knew I shouldn't have voted for that Jew."

I looked to see if Momma had overheard, but she kept her eyes on Daddy.

"I have always favored integration," he was saying. "That is no secret. I made it clear when I ran for this seat. Our country is changing," he concluded. "Blue Gap has to change with it."

Several folks jumped to their feet, all shouting at once. "If town council wants to support that nigger," a man yelled, "we'll just get ourselves another council!"

A woman cried, "And we don't need a Jew telling us how to live!"

Mr. Pearson banged on the table. "Order! Order!" I scooched my chair closer to Momma's; she reached out and took my hand.

The police chief stepped forward. "Sit down!" he barked. "Sit down, the lot of you!"

People took their seats. Mr. Pearson's face was flushed. "Y'all can raise your hands like civilized folks, or I will adjourn this meeting. Is that understood?"

Hands shot into the air again. Mr. Pearson nodded toward the back.

"Thank you, Mr. Pearson." I recognized the voice as belonging to Dr. Fuller, the town optometrist.

"Obviously there are a lot of feelings about this," he began. "However, Mr. Stern's point is a good one. Sooner or later our schools will have to integrate. It's the law of the land. I think a Negro policeman is a strong first step toward the inevitable. Council would do well to support it."

A few folks applauded; others booed. Momma squeezed my hand. Mr. Pearson called on a white-haired woman with clouded blue eyes.

She got up, leaning on a cane. "Blue Gap has always been a peaceful town. That's because folks knew their place."

She eyed my daddy. "Mr. Stern, when your grandfather came here to open his pajama factory, we didn't mind. There were Jews here already."

Her voice quavered. "But now you are going too far. You better watch your step, mister, that's all I've got to say."

A cold feeling washed over me. "I've heard enough,"

my mother said, rising and yanking me to my feet. "And so have you. Let's go."

"But, Momma," I protested. "What about Daddy?"

"He'll get a ride home," she answered. "Come on." And before I could get out another word, Momma had hustled me down the aisle and out the door.

The sky was inky and pocked with stars when Dr. Fuller's Chevrolet pulled into our driveway. I'd been sitting on the porch steps at least half an hour, flashlight in hand, waiting for my daddy to come home.

He got out and shut the door. "Good night, Ed," he said.

"What happened, Daddy?" I asked as he came up the walk.

He shook his head. "Council delayed the vote until the regular meeting in three weeks' time. I didn't want to wait that long. If they think I'll give up, they're mistaken."

Then he smiled down at me. "Want to sit out a while?"

I followed him to the backyard where we settled in the grass, leaning our backs against the sweetgum tree. The air was warm and still. The Milky Way spilled across the heavens, casting its pale spell on the world below. In the fields behind the house, fireflies danced above the tall grass, mirroring the sky.

High up sailed the kite-shaped constellation Bootes, pinned to the sky by the red star Arcturus. To the east flew Cygnus the Swan, neck extended, wings outspread. Below was Polaris, the constant North Star; nearby the seven bright points of the Big Dipper hung over the night-washed mountains.

My daddy had taught me the names of these stars. He'd showed me the path they made across the night, so I knew in what season they would disappear and when they would return. The universe was an immense clock that always ran on time.

Now he took my flashlight and swept its beam across the sky. "See those stars, Audrey Ina? That's where we come from. That's what we are."

"What do you mean, Daddy?"

"I mean everything you can lay your eyes on—the fields, those hills, the lightning bugs. All these things started out on one of those distant stars, millions and billions of years ago."

I squinted into the darkness. He went on. "You see, stars are kind of like people: They have a life. They're born, grow old, and die. And sometimes when they die, they explode."

He told me how other stars were made from the gas and dust of those explosions. And how, after a great long time, some of those new stars died and exploded. From them, more stars were born.

He said, "From the gas and dust of some dying star, our star, the Sun, was born. And the Earth and other planets were created at the same time, from that same gas and dust."

Nearly ninety-three million miles away from the Sun, life sprang up out of the Earth. It showed itself in so many ways; the fireflies in the fields were different from the mimosas in the front yard, but they both still pulsed with life. And Daddy and I, we were alive too.

"We're stardust, honey," my father mused. "Some

part of us began long ago on that distant star. And now here we are, sitting in the backyard together."

I could feel my heart beating. Under my knees cool blades of grass that had once been a star were sticking up and tickling me. The stars were very big and far away, but just then I felt like I could reach up and pull one into my lap.

"We're part of everything, Audrey," my father went on. "And everything is part of us. You, me, Tante, Mr. Cardwell—even the ones who hate us."

"You mean like those people tonight?"

He nodded. "Them too."

I frowned. "I don't see how you can say that, Daddy. Not after the things they said."

He looked at me. "Did they scare you?"

"A little," I admitted.

"They're angry, Audrey."

"Yeah, but they're angry about Mr. Cardwell wanting to be a policeman. What does that have to do with you being Jewish?"

"Nothing," he agreed. "But if a person hates, Audrey, they'll fling that hatred at whoever's in their way. Whether it's me or Mr. Cardwell, it doesn't matter."

I chewed a blade of grass, thinking about what he said. "Daddy?" I asked finally. "What's Kristallnacht?"

He cut his eyes at me. "You don't miss a thing, do you?"

I shrugged. "I never heard Tante mention it before."

"I know. She doesn't usually bring up the war, does she?" He sighed. "Some people say Kristallnacht was the real beginning of the war. For the Jews, anyway. It's a

German word meaning 'Crystal Night.' And it's the name for a night in 1938 when the Nazis smashed all the windows of all the shops in Germany that belonged to German Jews. On that night alone, tens of thousands of Jews were beaten—and many were killed."

"How awful. Only, Daddy, how can Tante think that one broken window is like Kristallnacht?"

"You have to see it through her eyes, Audrey." He thought a moment. "What a person lives through in the past can affect how they see the present. So something that may seem fairly small to you or me might, in Tante's mind, recall the war and appear bigger than it is. Does that make sense?"

"Sort of."

He hesitated. "Honey, I realize you and Tante aren't the best of friends."

"What you mean is she can't stand me."

"You're wrong, Audrey. Tante cares about you."

"Oh, sure, Daddy. And pigs can fly."

"I know she picks on you sometimes. Don't think I don't see it, because I do. But did you ever think maybe she's forgotten what it's like to be a kid?"

"She's not like that with Joel," I reminded him.

"Joel's a baby still," he answered, as if that explained everything. "Audrey, sometimes people go through such terrible things, they don't remember who they were before. You know Tante lost her entire family—"

"I know, Daddy. You've told me."

He eyed me. "But did you know everyone in Jarzyna was killed?"

I stared. "Everyone?"

"Tante was the only one, out of several hundred, to come through the war."

"How could they all die?"

Daddy's face was pale in the starlight. "Adolf Hitler was an evil man, Audrey. Maybe the worst the world has known. And he had it in his mind to destroy all the Jews in Europe."

"How come?"

"Oh, honey, if I knew the answer to that." He rubbed his face. "All I know is that when the Nazis invaded Poland, Hitler had his special police—the Gestapo—imprison the Jews in small, barbed-wire areas. Ghettoes, they're called.

"In the ghetto Tante was made to wear a yellow Star of David to show that she was Jewish. And these ghettoes were filthy places, with several families cramped in one room. There wasn't much to eat either, so a lot of people perished from sickness and starvation.

"Later, those that were still alive, like Tante and her family, were sent to Auschwitz and the other camps. There, anyone who looked like they weren't strong enough to work was killed in the gas chambers Hitler had built. Altogether, six million Jews died."

It was impossible to imagine the grim picture my father was painting. "Daddy, why are you telling me this now?"

"Believe me, Audrey," he answered. "I don't want to upset you any more than I have. The truth is, I'm worried about Tante. This thing with Mr. Cardwell could be hard on her. If there's more trouble, I'm afraid she might—" He broke off.

"She might what?"

He shook his head. "I just want you to understand why she acts the way she does."

"I understand, Daddy." Only it was a fib and we both knew it.

After a time he got to his feet. "You coming in?"

"Soon, okay?"

He leaned down to hug me. "Good night, Audrey Ina."

"Night, Daddy."

The kitchen door closed behind him, and the house stood quiet again. Tante's mournful eyes seemed to peer from its dark windows. I pushed them away and thought about the universe instead, filled with countless suns and stretching to forever.

3

When I woke up the next morning, there they were. During the night seven red bumps had broken out on my face, zigzagging from my eyebrow to my mouth.

I was brushing my teeth when I saw them. In the bathroom mirror they were small and raised, a little sore to the touch. If I leaned my head to the left, they took on the shape of a question mark. They reminded me of something else, but I could not think what—

The Big Dipper! These bumps were the exact shape of that constellation. Four of them cupped my eye; the rest were the handle, curving down my cheek.

My mind reeled. Supposing they were some kind of message? Or maybe even a sign. But where had they come from and what did they mean?

I knew about signs from talking to Frances Cardwell, our housekeeper. She believed in signs; The Bible was full of them. The Lord was always turning sticks into snakes or leaving a mark on somebody's forehead.

She must have heard me thinking about her, because her gravelly voice called up the stairs now. "Audrey Ina! Come on, child! You'll be late for services!"

I took one last look in the mirror before hurrying down. For once I was grateful for the galaxy of freckles flung across my face. They would hide these bumps from busybody eyes.

Frances was waiting at the bottom of the stairs, hands on her hips. A small woman, just an inch or two taller than me, she was bony as a chair. "What's that rash?" she asked, soon as she saw me.

"It's not a rash." I lowered my voice. "It may be a sign."

She threw back her head and laughed. "It's a sign, all right. It's a sign you got a rash."

Then she yanked me back up to the bathroom and sat me on the clothes hamper. She held my head with one hand, while the other dabbed witch hazel on my cheek. "What's this sign say?" she inquired. "Nobody home?"

"No, Frances. You know. Like in the Bible."

"The Bible?" Her hand stopped in midair. "Audrey Ina, what are you saying? Are you saying the Lord sent you a rash?" She put a hand on my forehead. "I hope you haven't got a fever."

"Does it look like anything to you?"

"Chicken pox."

"I've had chicken pox." I grabbed her birdy wrist. "What do you think it means?"

"It means you got a bad case of the make-believes." She leaned in to inspect the bumps. "They're probably just pimples," she declared. "Plain old ordinary pimples. That's all that's wrong with you, gal. You're growing up."

Before I could object, she pulled me to my feet. "Let's get you ready for *shul*." Shul meant "synagogue"; it was funny to hear Yiddish coming out of Frances.

Hands on my shoulders, she steered me into the hall. Daddy called up the stairs. "Time's a-wasting, Audrey Ina."

"We're bound for glory, Mr. Stern," Frances sang out.

In my room she pulled my Saturday dress out of the closet. While I buttoned it down, she whisked a brush through the red frazzle of my hair.

I looked in the mirror. The bumps faded into my freckles. Frances was right; it wasn't a sign, it was only a rash. Or maybe it *was* pimples.

Tante poked her head in, bangs rolled on metal curlers. "Frances, do you know where is my taffeta dress?"

"It's hanging in the laundry room, Miss Minkowitz." Frances always treated my aunt like she was made of glass. "I ironed it for you special."

"Thank you." Tante slid her eyes to me. "My God. Look at that hair."

I wrinkled my nose, in no mood to be teased about my hair. Frances tugged at a tangle. "It's in a knot this morning."

"No, no," my aunt replied distractedly. "It is gorgeous."

I was dumbstruck; Tante rarely paid me compliments. She came and took a curl between her fingers. "It is so like—" Her voice faded as a hand drifted to her curlers.

Then she saw my bumps and changed the subject. "What is this? Pimples?"

Frances chuckled. "She swears it's a sign."

Tante's eyes gleamed. "What kind of sign, please?"

"I'm not sure," I answered, shy under her gaze.

She gave me one of her uncommon smiles. "You believe in signs, Audrey?"

"I do. Don't you, Tante?"

Her eyes hardened. "I believe in nothing," she said, and turned out the door.

Frances watched her go too; our eyes met in the mirror. She glanced away. "Didn't expect to see you at the meeting last night," she murmured.

"I wish I hadn't gone now."

"I don't blame you for that." Handing me the brush, she began to make up the bed.

I watched her snap the sheet and sail it deftly down. "Frances? Can I ask you a personal question?"

She rolled her eyes. "Have I got a choice?"

"Do you hate working for white people?"

"Audrey Ina. The things that come out of your mouth."

"It *is* a conundrum," I agreed.

She smoothed the covers with brisk swipes. "You asking me something that can't be answered yes or no. The way your daddy is sticking his neck out for me and mine . . ." She shook her head.

"But you've worked for other white people," I persisted.

"Who else am I going to work for?" she flared. "Everything in this town belongs to one white man or another. Do I hate that? Yes, I do. Do I hate standing in the back of a white folks' meeting? You bet I do." She pursed her lips and started from the room.

"Frances, wait."

"Don't get me started on this now, Audrey." And she shook her head in a way that said this conversation was over.

* * *

Folks were already gathered in front of the synagogue when Daddy parked the car across the street. We joined the crowd, saying our hellos. Some twenty families belonged to the shul. We all pretty much knew one another's business; a body couldn't hardly get born or sick or die without everybody else hearing about it.

There were Gentiles on the sidewalk too, making their way to the stores. A Gentile is somebody who isn't Jewish, and that was most anybody in town. You could tell which ones thought it peculiar, us going to services on Saturday. For them, Saturday was for shopping, Sunday was for church.

The synagogue was a wooden storefront squeezed between Woolworth's five-and-dime on one side and the Paramount movie theater on the other. Friday nights we could hear the latest John Wayne movie coming through the walls during the rabbi's sermon. But Saturday morning services started at eight-thirty and Woolworth's didn't open till ten. Then the shul had a kind of hush to it. The bells on the Torah tinkled in the quiet when Daddy and my uncle Lewis lifted the scroll from the Holy Ark, the special cabinet where the Torah was stored.

Jews differ from Christians in that we don't worship Jesus as the Son of God. So we don't study the New Testament. The Torah is the five books of Moses from the Old Testament, written in Hebrew on thin yellow parchment. It's sacred and very old. Hearing it read every week gave me a shivery feeling.

"Baruch Ata Adonai Eloheinu Melech Ha'olam . . ." Rabbi Grody chanted in Hebrew. And the congregation

answered in a single voice: "Blessed art Thou, O Lord our God, King of the Universe."

The five of us sat together in a pew, Tante beside Joel, a black shawl hiding her face. When she prayed, her voice rose, thorny with grief.

Near the end of the service came the Kaddish, the Hebrew prayer for the dead. A Jewish person says Kaddish for eleven months after someone in their family has died; after that they say it once a year on the anniversary of the death.

Only Tante said Kaddish every time she came to shul. *"Yisgodal v'yisgodash sh'mei raba,"* she wailed, the words breaking against us. The congregation looked away and answered faintly, "Amen."

"Why does she have to say it every time?" I whispered to Daddy.

"If God doesn't mind," he whispered back, "neither should you."

When services were over, we drifted onto the sidewalk, blinking in the midmorning sun. I headed over to visit with June Silverman, my very best friend.

"Whew." June lifted her braids off her neck. "Makes me hot just to look at your aunt."

I glanced to where Tante stood in conversation with the rabbi. "She always wears black," I reminded her. "And long sleeves too. Even in August on the hottest dog days."

We knew why, though we hardly mentioned it anymore. The sleeves hid the line of blue numbers the Nazis had tattooed on Tante's arm in Auschwitz. They'd always been there, strange and also familiar.

I got off the subject. "Did you hear about Mr. Cardwell?" I asked.

"Uh-huh." June looked uninterested. Then, grabbing my arm, she exclaimed, "Oh, I near forgot! Look what my cousin Beth sent for my birthday."

She twirled a tiny Star of David hung on a chain around her neck. The six-pointed star was delicate and made of gold.

I put my nose skyward. "Guess we'll have to forgive her now."

We looked at each other and busted out laughing. June's cousin Beth was from New York City. She visited Blue Gap last summer and never tired of reminding us that she was a Yankee and we were rebels.

There was the time she'd told Frances that if the Yankees had not won the Civil War, Frances would still be a slave. Frances had looked at Beth like she might be slightly cuckoo. Then she did a funny thing: She stopped hanging sheets on the clothesline long enough to shake the girl's hand.

June settled beside me on the steps now. "You know what Beth told me? Nearly everybody on her block is Jewish."

"She's lying like a rug." Nobody on our road was Jewish except us.

"I swear, Audrey. She said her whole school lets out for Rosh Hashanah and Yom Kippur." Those were the High Holy Days that came in autumn. "They don't have to bring in an excuse note for being absent."

Where I went to elementary school in the county, I was the only Jewish kid. And even June's school in town had only six Jewish students.

"I like bringing in an excuse," I fibbed. "Makes me feel special."

June's eyes darted behind me. I felt my aunt's shadow before I saw it, eclipsing mine on the sidewalk.

"Good Shabbos, Tante Pesel," June said, politelike.

"*Shabbat shalom,*" my aunt replied; that meant "Sabbath peace."

She had Joel in tow. "Hey, June." Brother grinned, finger up his nose. My aunt tweaked it, making him giggle.

"Tante, I just love your dress," my friend gushed.

Even I couldn't deny it was beautiful. She'd made it herself out of fine taffeta, painstakingly sewing glass beads into the neck and sash. The flared skirt showed off her slender waist.

Her eyes shone. "You are saying this because it is true."

June laughed. Tante reached out and tapped her new Star of David. "And what is this, please?"

"My cousin sent it," June replied. "They're all the rage in New York City."

"That is quite interesting. What means 'all the rage'?"

"Fashionable," I told her.

"Ah." Her eyes darkened. "Go find me Lewis, yes? I am going to the car with Brother."

"She can be so charming," June whispered, as the two crossed the street.

By the time I gave my uncle Tante's message, June was nowhere to be found. So I went and sat on the curb near Momma and Daddy.

In the car my aunt lit a cigarette; a rope of smoke circled her head. I watched as Uncle Lewis talked to her through the open window. My father's younger brother, Uncle Lewis, was one of two dentists in town. His office had a lot of swell gadgets in it; one squirted Dr Pepper in your mouth if you had a good checkup. Squat and round, always sporting a bow tie, Uncle Lewis kind of reminded me of a penguin.

The sun bore down, making me drowsy. The voices on the sidewalk melted into one pleasant hum. I'd nearly dozed off when I heard my uncle say: "Heard you had a little party at the courthouse last night."

My eyes popped open. Uncle Lewis was standing with my folks now. "If you two will excuse me," my mother said. "Shabbat shalom, Lewis." She kissed his cheek and joined my aunt and Joel in the car.

"Is that what you were talking to Tante about?" my father asked him, sending an anxious look in her direction.

Uncle Lewis nodded. "She wanted to know what I'd heard. She's scared, Nathan."

"I know she is."

My uncle scratched his head. "And you're still determined to go through with this?"

"I am."

Uncle Lewis shook his head. "Then it's true what people are saying. You have completely taken leave of your senses."

Daddy did not respond, so my uncle kept on. "Nathan, it's all well and good for you and Cardwell to dream. But this will backfire in your face. I mean it. Why do you have to be the one to push it?"

Daddy looked him in the eye. "You know why."

"No, I don't!" Uncle Lewis exploded. "Explain it to me."

"All right, hush." My father took his brother by the sleeve and pulled him down the sidewalk.

I got up and inched behind them, hanging in the shade of the building to listen. Daddy dropped his voice. "How long have I lived with Tante now? Ten, eleven years? And every time I look at her, what do I see? I see a girl whose life was utterly ripped apart by hatred—"

My uncle broke in, whispering fiercely. "Oh, and have you considered what this might do to her? It could open up all her old wounds. For God's sake, Nathan, hasn't she suffered enough?"

"Mr. Cardwell's suffering, Lewis. He's a victim of hatred too."

My uncle sighed. "Nat, please, I'm begging you. Don't make trouble for the rest of us. So far we Jews have been left alone in peace. You go stirring things up, all that could change."

My daddy thrust his hands in his pockets. "And what about my children? How else do I teach them right from wrong unless I do what I believe is right myself?"

He turned then, starting for the car. I dashed out in front of him. Uncle Lewis called after us, "It's your children I'm worried about."

4

The conversation between my father and my uncle stayed with me on the ride home from shul. I sat in the back with Tante, Joel slouched against her, asleep. She stared out one window; I stared out the other.

Smoke from the paper mills hung over the town, caught in the gap between the mountains. Some folks likened the smell to rotten eggs, others to boiled cabbage; either way, it stank. I hardly noticed it, though, as we drove through downtown. Fact was, Blue Gap had two downtowns—one for whites, one for Negroes—separated as cleanly as two cut pieces of cloth.

On Church Street in the white downtown, brick buildings lined hilltops overlooking the James River. Whites moved along like they had someplace to be, and every once in a while a Negro passed silently among them.

The courthouse square was planted with neat summer rows of red, white, and blue petunias. The fragile blossoms of a magnolia sent perfume over benches where old men in straw hats dozed in the sun. Under its shade were two water fountains. One had a sign "Whites Only"; the other read "Colored."

Once when I was five, I took a sip from the colored fountain. I told my daddy I wanted to see what colored water tasted like. He explained the water was the same in each; the signs were for people, not water.

Now we turned onto Fifth Street, the Negro downtown. Here was a restaurant, a funeral parlor, a rundown movie theater. The storefronts were small and bunched together; many needed paint. No doubt about it, Fifth Street was shabbier than Church. Of course it made sense, since Negroes couldn't make any money at the jobs they were permitted to do. I figured a policeman had to be a better-paid job.

We weren't rich, but we were better off than the Cardwells. Still, I was starting to see how some folks in Blue Gap really felt about us Jews. There had always been signs. Even though we drank from the white water fountain, I knew there were places we weren't allowed either. The Sycamore Country Club was one.

I'd found that out in third grade, when my classmate Edwina Clark had her birthday party there. Edwina and I weren't exactly friends, but usually every girl got invited to every other girl's party, whether you were friends or not; that was how it was done.

One morning in school the girls were atwitter. They'd gotten their invitations in the mail the day before. Mine hadn't come yet, and when I learned where the party was being held, I knew it never would.

At first I felt punched in the stomach. But by the time recess rolled around, I was starting to fume. I marched across the blacktop to Edwina. "I didn't want to go to your old party anyhow," I told her flat out.

"Well, that's good." Edwina had light green eyes and stick-straight blond hair. "Because you couldn't if you wanted to."

"Oh, who gives a hoot about your stupid country club?"

"How do you know it's stupid? You've never been there."

"I don't see why I can't go."

"Because, Audrey. You're Jewish."

"So?"

"So, you haven't been baptized. You're going to burn forever in you-know-where."

I rolled my eyes. "Edwina, Jesus was Jewish."

"Says who?"

"They told us so in Sunday school."

"Well." She bit her lip. "Nobody's perfect."

"Oh!" I stamped my foot. "Jesus couldn't care less about your dumb old country club! And neither do I!" And I whirled away.

But I *did* care. And it was hard holding up my head in front of the other girls, pretending I didn't. The day of the party came and went, and pretty soon things seemed to go back to normal. I ate my lunch with everybody again and traded my moon pies like always.

Only it was never the same. I couldn't shake that hollow feeling that came from being left out. The other girls belonged; I didn't. There was something about me that marked me as different.

By the time we got home from shul, my head was aching. So when Momma said what she needed was a long, cool soak at the swimming hole, I said, "Count me in."

After lunch we threw on our bathing suits and banged out the kitchen door. Cutting through the back fields, Joel ran ahead of Momma and me, chasing after grasshoppers. He led us through a patch of woods, following a narrow stream.

At last we came to where the creek widened and a low waterfall fell into a calm pocket of water. Weeping willows spread their roots at the pool's edge. On the other side a rope swing had been tied to the limb of a red maple. On hot days there were plenty of kids here, mostly from my school. But this afternoon it was empty. Joel couldn't swim yet, so he was happy to stay on the bank, sifting through the muck for small hidden creatures.

Momma and I walked along the top of the waterfall and slid into the pool. The water was startlingly cold. We swam back and forth, laughing and splashing. Then we sat under the falls, letting the curtain of water hit our heads and roll down.

Afterward Momma sunned on a rock near Brother, while I swung on the rope again and again. Finally she sat up. "I'm going to burn to a crisp if I sit here any longer. Let's go, y'all."

"Not yet, Momma," I begged. "Can't I stay a while? Please?"

Joel jumped up and down. "Me too, me too?"

"Well, I guess it'd be all right. Fifteen minutes and straight home, hear me?"

After she left, I paddled around some, then floated on my back, drifting toward the other side. The sun was hot on my face. Far off I could hear the faint rattle of a kingfisher; closer by came Joel's splashes and cries of delight.

Something went *kerplunk!* beside me. I started up, peering into the churning water, the rope swinging above me. "Who was that, Joel?"

A hand grabbed my foot, trying to pull me under. I kicked away. A face bobbed to the surface; it belonged to Buster LaCoste, a boy from my fifth grade.

Some girls thought Buster was cute, with his long eyelashes and wavy sideburns, but he had the brains of a potato. The joke around school was that Buster had been held back in the fifth grade more times than he could count. One winter he put weasel glands on the school's heating pipes and they had to close the building for two whole days just to let the stink out. That was about the brightest thing that boy ever did.

Now I splashed water at him. "I should have known it was you."

He grinned. "Sorry, Red."

"Only you are dumb enough to call me that."

He gargled water and squirted it out. Glancing back toward Brother, I saw two other boys sitting on the bank near him. I guessed they were friends of Buster's. Like him, they were a few years older than me and probably went to the junior high.

I started for shore. "Hey, Red, where you going?" Buster yelled.

"I came here for some peace and quiet," I said over my shoulder. "Guess that was a dream."

"Aw, don't leave because of us."

I turned on my back to watch him climb the far bank. He reached up and grabbed the rope swing, a long ragged scar flashing on his arm. He pulled the rope back as far as it would go. Then he ran toward the creek, swinging out over it and yodeling like Tarzan the Apeman, "Aah-*ahh*-ahh-*ahh*-ahhhhh," before dropping in.

He bobbed up near me, squirting out water in my direction. "Me Tarzan, you Jane," he said.

I rolled my eyes. "Me Jane, you Cheetah." Cheetah was Tarzan's pet chimpanzee.

His friends guffawed. The biggest of the two boys had a bad case of acne. He looked at me and said, "Buster told us your daddy's the Jew trying to help that nigger."

Right away I wished we'd gone home with Momma. I started backkicking toward Joel. Buster dove under and came up between me and the shore.

"My cousin saw you at the meeting last night, Red," he smirked, dog-paddling toward me. "Sitting by the niggers."

My heart began to pound. Behind him I could see Joel watching us. Buster taunted, "I knew your daddy was a nigger lover, Red. Didn't take you for one too."

"I'd rather love a Negro than a moron like you. Now get out of my way." I lunged forward, but he wouldn't let me pass. I tried diving under, but his foot found my head and pushed my face into the bottom. Wriggling free, I got up sputtering. My hand went to my forehead and came away with clay and blood on it.

"Go home, Joel." I tried to sound calm. "Go on. You know the way."

He hesitated. "But, Audie—"

"Do as I say!" I shouted, and Brother burst out crying.

Buster turned to him. "Aw, kid, don't do that."

"I'd be crying too," the boy with acne said, "if my daddy was as stupid as his."

That made Joel wail harder. "Shut that kid up," the other boy grumbled.

"Leave him alone," I said.

"Audie." Brother held out his arms to me.

"I'm coming, Joel." My voice shook. "Just let us go home, okay, Buster?"

Buster glanced at the others, unsure what to do. The pimple-faced boy jumped to his feet. "I'll shut that kid up." He strode over and lifted Joel up by his hands.

"Audie!" Brother shrieked.

"Put him down!" I cried.

The boy sneered. "Here's what we do to Jews that get out of line." He swung Joel up and dangled him above the falls. Terrified, Brother kicked and screamed.

"He can't swim!" I yelled at Buster. "Make your friend stop!"

Buster frowned. "Put him down," he called to the boy.

"Okay," the boy said, grinning, and dropped Joel into the falls.

"No!" I shrieked.

The water bounced Brother on his back into the pool. I started toward him, but he disappeared beneath the swirling water. "Joel!"

Buster dove down as Brother bobbed to the surface, still on his back. I caught him and he clung to me, coughing and crying.

"Leave us alone!" My voice was ragged. "Just leave us alone!"

Buster scrambled out of the water and into the woods, the other boys behind him. I carried Joel to shore. "It's okay, Brother. You're okay." Then we sank in a heap, me rocking him, till his sobs quieted to hiccups.

I gave Brother a piggyback ride home. In the yard Tante was resting in the hammock. We started past her without a word.

"Wait," she called. "What happen to your face?"

"I fell," I fibbed, not turning around. "Where is everybody?"

"Your *tata* went out." Tata was Polish for "father." "Your momma is napping. Why is Brother so quiet?"

"He's sleepy," I replied, and hurried into the house.

In the kitchen I fixed Joel some lemonade. "Don't tell anybody what happened," I told him. "I'll tell them myself when I get back."

He peered over the rim of his glass. "Where you going, Audie?"

"Never mind. Just promise me, okay?"

He nodded. We found Frances downstairs in the laundry room. Joel settled on the floor beside her, watching ants cross the cool cement.

I slipped out of the house. Part of me wanted to get on my bike and ride as far away from Blue Gap as I could. But another part needed to understand how this could be happening to us.

I headed for the factory.

5

Stern's Nightwear and Company was a three-story brick building with flashing tin roofs and thundering doors. Rows of skinny windows caught the afternoon light; on the third floor a square of cardboard had been taped behind the shattered pane.

As I looked up at it, I heard Tante saying, *This window is the beginning.* It made me shiver, though the sun was hot on my shoulders.

I rode around back to where a fire escape crisscrossed the brick. Three wet mopheads dripped from the lowest landing. Mr. Cardwell leaned beside them. Though the factory was closed today, like every Saturday, he always came in to wind the clocks and wash the floors.

"Hey, Mr. Cardwell," I called up. "Thought I might find you here."

Mr. Cardwell was a big man, large as Frances was small. He had a broad handsome face and thick veiny arms. I tried to imagine him in a tan policeman's uniform; I'd seen the picture Frances kept of him in her wallet as a corporal in World War II.

"Howdy, Audrey," he called back. "What you doing here?"

I politely ignored his question, busy wondering how to pose my own. Grown-ups could be slippery if you asked them things outright.

"Mighty quiet" was all I could come up with.

Flies buzzed. Mr. Cardwell was what's known as the strong, silent type. He was a man of few words, but Daddy said every one of them counted.

"Mr. Cardwell?" I began again. "Can I ask you a personal question? How come you want to be a policeman?"

Mr. Cardwell kept his eyes out over the river. "I was a soldier in the war," he said at last. "Like your daddy, I fought for my country."

"Only he was in the army, and you were a marine," I threw in.

What he didn't say was something else I knew. Mr. Cardwell had been decorated for bravery in combat. Now he kept his hero's medal on a stand in his living room, surrounded by tiny American flags.

He went on. "After the war I came back to Blue Gap and wouldn't nobody give me a job. Except for small stuff, like hauling firewood and raking leaves. I got a wife and children, and I couldn't put bread on my table."

"That's not right," I protested.

"That's when Mr. Stern give me this job. Lots of folks resented him for that, Audrey, but he did it just the same. We both knew then I could do more than what this job is. Now I want that chance."

"But if you're the reason that window got broke—?"

"Not the first time something's been thrown at me."

"And you aren't scared?"

"You get used to scared. After a while, it's not a good enough reason to sit and do nothing. You know what I mean?"

"I guess."

Mr. Cardwell squinted at the sun. "Time to pick up the missus." He tilted his head at me. "Mr. Stern know you're here?"

"No, sir."

"You best get on home then." And tipping his hat, he hurried on inside.

I didn't go home like Mr. Cardwell told me; I went to the library instead. The Blue Gap Public Library was where I went whenever I was confused or bothered in my mind. And all I wanted right then was to curl up with a book in some dusty corner and forget about everything.

The library was lined with shelves and hung with portraits of famous Virginians in wigs. The whole place smelled of mildew, ammonia, and Miss Farley's gardenia perfume.

Henrietta Farley was the librarian. Rumor had it she hemmed her skirts with safety pins. Her hair was mussed this way and that, and her glasses sat crookedly on her nose. She smiled over them as I passed her desk, beelining for the nonfiction.

I pulled out a faded brown volume all about astronomy, the science of the stars. The book was so old and worn, it couldn't be checked out of the library anymore. Still, I'd sat in a chair and traveled with it many afternoons through the big comforting emptiness of space.

The frontispiece was a photo of Dr. Albert Einstein, a scientist from Germany who was Jewish like us. He had died just last year, an old man with wild hair and deep, soft eyes. Dr. Einstein changed the way people thought about time. He said there is really no such thing as time, not as we measure it in seconds, minutes, and hours. Because time behaves differently depending on your speed.

Dr. Einstein believed the speed of light to be the one thing in the universe that never changes. It's always the same—186,000 miles *a second*—no matter where the light comes from or how far it goes. He also said something I didn't really understand: that if you could travel at that speed, the watch on your wrist would appear to tick more slowly, at least to someone moving at usual human speed.

That got me thinking. So much had happened in just one day; it was hard to believe it was only yesterday the window got broke. Maybe it was like Dr. Einstein's theory: When things moved quickly, time had appeared to me to slow down.

I flipped through the book till I came on a drawing of the Big Dipper. The constellation was about seventy-five light-years away, a light-year being the distance light travels in one year. It measures space, not time.

I felt along my face; the bumps were still there. And then a crazy notion danced into my head. Suppose someone out in space had seen Daddy's and my flashlight beam the night before? And these bumps, coming while I slept, were their way of telling me they had received our signal? It was possible, I told myself. The universe was a mysterious place. Things went on in it nobody understood, not even Dr. Einstein—

"Shh!" went a voice by my ear, making me jump. The librarian peered at me through cockeyed glasses. "I can hear you thinking, Audrey, you're thinking so hard."

"Miss Farley?" I asked flat out. "Do you believe there's intelligent life in outer space?"

She plopped down beside me. "I certainly hope it's intelligent. We need all the help we can get."

"Well, wouldn't you love to go and find out?"

She looked at me aghast. "Who'd feed my cats?"

I giggled; it was common knowledge that Miss Farley was unusually fond of her six cats. "You know what I mean. Wouldn't it be neat to go far, far away? Just sail off into the galaxy and never have to worry about anything again."

She humphed. "What don't you want to worry about?"

"Nothing." It didn't come out very sincere.

"I was at the courthouse last night, Audrey."

I gaped. "You must be a mind reader, Miss Farley. Only I didn't see you there."

"I didn't have much to say." She stood up. "Come with me. I want to show you something."

I followed her out back to the garden where sunlight filled the cups of roses and azaleas. Finches bickered in a mossy birdbath beside stone benches sitting patiently under dogwoods white with flowers. Pin oaks led to an abandoned field bordered by stone walls. Tangles of honeysuckle and raspberry vine sprouted up through piles of tumbledown wood.

"You know that the library used to be the main house of an old tobacco plantation, don't you?" Miss Farley asked me now.

"Oh yes, ma'am," I answered. "Before the Civil War."

She nodded. "Well, those rotting heaps of wood out there are all that remain of the shacks where Negro slaves once lived."

I stared. We'd studied about slavery in fifth grade, but standing by those ruins suddenly made it come alive. I tried to picture how the cabins might have looked, squatting in the shadow of the big house, with peeling tar-paper roofs.

Miss Farley went on. "Mr. Cardwell's great-grandmother was born in one of those."

"Really?"

"Yes. Lived there her whole life."

"How do you know?"

"We have the old county slave rolls in the library," she replied. "At one time her parents, she and her husband, and their five children all lived together. Nine people crammed into a one-room shack."

Her words put me in mind of the ghetto where Tante had been forced to live. "Oh, Miss Farley, don't you wish you could make those piles disappear? Just like that." I waved my arms. "Abracadabra."

"Not me, Audrey," she replied. "I want them to stay as long as they can. I think if I could, I'd rebuild them."

"Whatever for?"

"So we wouldn't forget it happened." She thought a moment. "Mr. Cardwell's great-grandmother worked in the main house all her life. Now his children are not permitted inside the library. I can't tell you how that tears me up."

Her lips wrinkled like she might cry. "Your father's a brave man, Audrey. Mr. Cardwell too. Flying in the face of hatred and prejudice. I wish I had their courage."

"So do I," I admitted.

She patted me absently. "They say courage is contagious. Maybe we'll catch some."

I grinned. "Miss Farley, I cannot remember when I've had a more illuminating conversation with a grown-up."

It was after five when I got home. Lacy shadows fell across the yard. Tante was waiting for me on the porch, her face white. The car was gone.

"Where have you been?" she demanded.

"At the library. Tante, what's wrong?"

She stubbed out her cigarette. "You had your momma worried."

"How come?"

She turned into the house without answering. I followed behind. Brother stood on the stairs, fingers in his mouth.

"Joel, shoo, go up and play," Tante said.

In the kitchen she began to fix a glass of iced coffee. She struck a match to light the stove; the flame quivered in her hand.

"Tante, what's going on? Where is everybody?"

She glared. "You do not fool me, Audrey Ina. I know something is wrong. I ask Brother what happen at creek. He tells me what he can and I tell Selma."

My heart sank. I didn't say anything.

"When Mr. Cardwell picks up Frances, he mentions he sees you at factory. You do not come home and Selma gets nervous. They go in the car to look for you."

The kettle clattered on the stove. "It is so easy for

you," she went on. "You go here, you go there. You have not yet learned to fear."

"I'm catching on fast," I told her.

"Not fast enough," she replied.

She tensed, listening, as the Studebaker pulled into the driveway. Rushing to the window, she called out, "She is here, Selma, she is fine."

"We know," Daddy called back. "We saw Henny Farley walking home."

They came in, sinking down at the table. Momma pointed me to a chair. "Start at the beginning, young lady. What exactly happened at the swimming hole?"

By the time I'd finished, my mother was pale. "This is my fault. I knew better than to leave you there alone."

"But, Audrey, why didn't you tell somebody when you got home?" Daddy demanded.

"I wanted to go to the factory. And I knew if I told Momma, she wouldn't let me."

"So you just took off without telling anyone where you were going?"

"Yes, sir."

He frowned. "Look, I realize you're a big girl and you're used to doing what you please. But things are different this summer. From now on there will be no more riding your bike all over town."

"*What?*"

"You heard me. Up and down Westerly Drive is fine. But downtown and the river are off-limits. And so is the creek."

I couldn't believe my ears. "Daddy, I'll be more careful, I promise. Please, pretty please? I've got to have *some* fun."

Momma said, "Audrey, we have to know that we can trust you."

Tante's voice came hard. "You cannot trust her, Selma. She does not understand."

I turned to her. "What don't I understand?"

Her eyes darted away; she didn't answer. Daddy said, "She's right, Audrey. You stay close to home this summer."

I slunk down, afraid I'd start crying. "I hate this."

Momma held out her hands. "Audrey, come here." I climbed onto her lap, too big for it really. She put her arms around me. "We're all in this together."

"Nobody asked me," I sulked.

The kettle howled. My aunt put a spoon in a glass and poured boiling water over it. The steam rose, filling the room and clouding the windows, so that for the moment we could not see out.

6

That night the stars seemed to be calling me. When the house grew dark, I went out into the yard, aiming the flashlight at the Big Dipper, wishing its beam was a ladder I could climb to those winking, faraway lights.

Blinking it on and off, again and again, I signaled the stars. *Here I am. Come and get me.*

I sighed. Even traveling at the speed of light, it wasn't hard to figure out that it would take my puny beam at least seventy-five years to get there. And even supposing there was someone there to receive it, I'd still be as old as Grandma Lena before it ever arrived.

I turned it off. Bat shadows flickered in the darkness, following echoes. The moon came up, flat on one side, and chased away the stars.

Tante's lamp came on, casting a dim rectangle outside her open window. From where I sat, I could see the top of her head, moving back and forth across the room. I crawled on my hands and knees through the wet grass to see what she was doing. Stopping at the light's edge, I watched her pace feverishly inside, wringing her hands.

After a time she reached under her bed and pulled out a small wooden box. Lifting the lid, she took out a tiny object. It appeared to be some kind of handmade figure, with string for hair. She smoothed the hair down. "Pesel, poor Pesel," she murmured. "What have they done to you?"

Who was she talking to? Pesel was *her* name. She returned the doll to its box and placed it back under the bed. Her face was a mask of sorrow when she turned out the light.

I didn't tell anyone what I'd seen, but the sight of my aunt bent over the little doll stuck in my mind. Where had it come from? Who had made it? Had she carried it with her all the way from Jarzyna? And why had she called it Pesel?

I wondered if my folks knew of it, only I was not about to ask. Momma had taken to going around with a worried look on her usually merry face, and my father was hardly ever home.

A few nights later Daddy informed me that rather than wait for town council to vote again, he and Mr. Cardwell had decided to speak to the police chief in person. They wanted to keep the meeting hush-hush, so it was best if no one knew exactly when and where it would be.

A week crept by. The bumps on my face faded. The spokes on my bike gathered cobwebs. Each night I slipped into the yard, but Tante's light did not go on again.

One morning I awoke to a sputtering out back. I leaped from the bed and threw on my clothes. Sam Cardwell was here to mow the grass. Tall, skinny, and lightning-quick, Sam was going to play junior varsity football come fall for Dunbar High School where the Negro teenagers went. I ran out barefoot to where he was bent, pouring gasoline into the mower. "Hey, Sam."

He didn't look up. "Hey, yourself."

I stopped in my tracks. Sam's right eye was swollen shut and he had a nasty cut on his lower lip. "Oh, no," I gasped. "What happened to you?"

"Bunch of white boys jumped me." He worked up some saliva and spit. "Guess they figure they got a reason now."

I followed him back to the toolshed. Watching him heave the gas can onto a shelf, I muttered, "Maybe this policeman business isn't such a hot idea."

"Bite your tongue, girl," Sam replied. "It'd take more than a black eye to make my daddy quit. Shoot, they bombed those folks in Montgomery, that didn't stop them."

My father had told me about the Negroes in that Alabama city. Like them, Blue Gap Negroes had to ride in the back of the bus, segregated from white folks. Only in Montgomery, the Negroes had refused to ride at all, till the bus company would allow them to sit wherever they pleased. The bus boycott had started last December; nearly six months later, it was still going on.

"Don't you think it's strange we haven't seen a word about the boycott in the *Advance*?" I asked Sam now. *The Daily Advance* was the town's morning newspaper.

"That's a white folks' paper, Audrey," he chided. "They're not about to pay attention to Negro news. Might make it seem important."

Frances threw open a window. "Audrey Ina! You leave that child alone. He's got work to do."

"I'm not bothering him," I returned.

"Don't tell me." She drew her head in.

Sam snorted. "Maw's jumpy this morning."

I slid my eyes at him. "Is today the day?"

"Shh." He nodded yes.

"Really." I lowered my voice. "You know what time?"

"Two thirty," he whispered.

"Where?"

"Police station. Maw's going," he added.

"Boy, I'd like to be a fly on the wall for that one."

"Shoot, they might not even get in the door."

"You reckon?"

"I don't guess the police chief's putting out the welcome mat, Audrey."

"You think someone could get hurt?" Sam shrugged in answer. "Are you going?" I asked him.

"Uh-uh, not me," he declared. "I got parade practice."

"Then you're still going to march in it?"

His good eye lit up. "Does a chicken have lips?"

The parade he meant was the Fourth of July parade, Blue Gap's annual to-do. It started out in front of the library, curled through both downtowns, and ended at the river. Folks showed up in all kinds of outlandish costumes; one time the whole Presbyterian junior choir came dressed like tomatoes. There were clowns and majorettes, floats and marching bands too.

Two years ago the Dunbar band had been permitted to join the parade, so long as they took up the rear. This year their football teams were planning to march behind the band in their uniforms.

Sam's grin was lopsided. "Maw says I look like a lollipop in my helmet."

I snickered. "I'd even pay money to see that."

Frances poked her head out again, and this time Sam jumped. "Catch you later, Audrey Ina." He pulled the cord on the mower and took off behind it, showers of grass arcing alongside.

All that morning I tried to imagine Daddy and the Cardwells showing up at the police station. I couldn't help worrying about what was going to happen. By lunchtime I was determined to get there any way I could. But first I had to get past Momma.

I found her in her bedroom, putting up her hair. My parents' room was sundrenched and cheerful, with photos of our family on the walls. Her dressing table had snapshots on it too, and all kinds of knickknacks.

"Going someplace, Momma?"

She drew a ragged breath. "I've got a sisterhood meeting at shul. Frances has to leave early, so you and Brother'll have to come with me."

"How long will we be, you think?"

"Oh, two hours at the most."

I watched her brush her hair with swift, nervous strokes. "Are you worried about Daddy?" I asked.

Her eyes flickered to mine in the mirror. "Let's just say I'll be glad when this situation with Mr. Cardwell is resolved."

"You could stop him if you wanted to," I ventured.

"Well, between you and me, honey, I wouldn't have him any other way." She tossed her head, smooth ribbons of hair catching the light. "Tell you the truth, I'm more worried about Tante than I am him."

I played with the nap of her bedspread. "Isn't she the reason he's helping Mr. Cardwell?"

She turned to face me. "What makes you so smart?"

"You can learn a lot eavesdropping, Momma."

The corners of her mouth twitched. "I'll keep that in mind."

"Daddy told me about Jarzyna and everybody getting killed."

"It's unreal, isn't it?"

"Uh-huh."

"Gets real mighty quick though, when you live with a person. God, Audrey, if you had seen her when she first came here, you wouldn't have recognized her."

"What was she like?"

Momma curled her lip, thinking. "Silent and fearful. She had these big empty eyes, like she was hollow and dead inside. She'd been out of the concentration camp only a few months."

She pushed my hair back off my forehead. "She didn't have hardly any hair. The Nazis had shaved her head. And she was horribly thin—they'd starved her down to skin and bones. I don't think she weighed more than fifty pounds."

"At thirteen?"

"Well, think about it, honey. She was a prisoner almost two years."

I did the arithmetic in my head and discovered with a pang that my aunt had been eleven when she went into Auschwitz. She'd been just my age.

I turned to myself in the mirror. What would I look

like, head shaved, thin as a skeleton?

"How come she wasn't killed like everybody else?" I asked.

Momma shook her head. "I don't know. Seems like a miracle, doesn't it?"

A hummingbird thrummed at the window and darted away. My mother turned back to the mirror, gathering her hair in a knot. The conversation had not gone at all the way I expected.

I banged my legs against the bed. "Momma? Do I have to come with you to the meeting?"

"What? You want to stay home? By yourself?"

"It won't be by myself," I replied. "Sam'll be here a while more."

She eyed me in the mirror. "What'll you do?"

"I don't know. Read or something. Anything'd be better than that boring old meeting."

"I'm kind of partial to boring myself." Momma opened bobby pins with her teeth and stuck them in her hair. "Well," she said finally. "I guess that sounds harmless enough."

At one thirty Mr. Cardwell came and picked up Frances. Shortly after, Momma and Brother left also. I tucked my hair under a floppy hat, put on a pair of my mother's swank sunglasses, counted out some change, and walked down to the bus stop. Nobody had to tell me what I was doing was sneaky. At least I wasn't adding insult to injury by disobeying Daddy and riding my bike.

I had two whole hours. More than enough time to get downtown, see my daddy safely inside the station house, and hurry on home, with no one the wiser.

7

I had to admit I liked riding the bus. The fare box chattered happily when I dropped my dime in it, and it was interesting to bump along the city streets and watch the people getting on and off. The bus was nearly empty, so instead of picking a seat in the middle like I usually did, I took myself to the back where the Negroes had to sit. I was curious to see how that felt.

For one thing, it was stuffier in back, with the fumes from the engine going right up my nose. The bus looked longer from there; the center aisle opened up down front, where the seats turned to face each other, making more room for whites.

On Fifth Street, a Negro woman got on and started for the back. A white man had his legs stuck out in the aisle. He didn't bother to move them, so she had to step over them. Each pretended like the other wasn't there; they were good at it too.

When the bus let me off, the courthouse clock said twenty after two. I tore over to the police station, a two-story brick building with barred windows on top. Neither our car nor the Cardwells' was anywhere to be seen.

Inside, the station house was surprisingly quiet and pleasantly cool. Fans whirred overhead. Behind a desk a man with a squared-off crew cut leafed through a magazine; a hound whimpered in her sleep at his feet.

Frances sat on a bench nearby, hands clasping her purse. She looked tiny and out of place, her shoulders set in that determined way she had.

"Help you, little lady?" the man drawled at me.

I drew back, hoping to hide behind Momma's sunglasses, but Frances recognized me. "Audrey Ina, what in the world—?" She slapped her knee. "Uh-uh, no, ma'am. You turn right around, Miss Noseytoes. You got no business here."

I had to talk fast. "I thought I'd keep you company."

"You thought wrong."

I looked around. "Where's Daddy?"

"They just went in. Now get yourself home."

"Is there a problem?" the crew cut asked.

Frances tensed. "No, sir." But her eyes were telling me otherwise.

Seeing I was getting nowhere fast, I turned back down the stairs. Running along the front of the building, I darted into a side alleyway lined with garbage cans.

Voices came out a window above me. I recognized Daddy's, and the one that sounded like a bullfrog had to be Mr. Monroe's. There were only those battered cans to stand on, but the lids seemed sturdy. I stuck my sunglasses in a pocket and climbed up on one, balancing against the brick. On my tippytoes I could just peer over the windowsill.

Luckily no one was facing me head-on. Mr. Monroe sat sideways behind a desk ten feet away. Across from him sat my father, Mr. Cardwell, and Reverend Hutcherson. The air between the four men felt starched.

The reverend's black suit shone from so many pressings. "We appreciate you seeing us today, Mr. Monroe," he intoned.

Whoosh ping! The police chief spat tobacco juice into a can at his feet. Frown lines made a gully in his forehead. "I am not a happy man," he croaked.

Mr. Cardwell spoke in his plain way. "I want this job, Mr. Monroe. I'm a hard worker."

"I'll vouch for that," my daddy chimed in.

Mr. Monroe filled his cheek with a wad of chaw. "We all know your record, Mr. Cardwell. And your character. You're qualified. That ain't the point."

"It's exactly the point, Elmo," my father returned.

The police chief shifted his big bulk. "Tell me something, Nat Stern. What in the name of sanity are you doing here?"

My daddy grinned. "I'm doing my civic duty. Recruiting a good man for your police force."

"Don't do me any favors." *Whoosh ping!* "I got two other applications for this job on my desk. Give me one good reason why I should hire Mr. Cardwell."

"Because you're not going to find a better man and you know it," Daddy answered.

"Let's talk plain, okay?" the police chief said. "It's my job to keep the peace in Blue Gap."

"Mr. Monroe, we're not looking for a fight. We're looking for what's fair; we're looking for what's right," Reverend Hutcherson replied.

"What's right for you, Reverend," Mr. Monroe boomed, "may not be right for me. See, I look at what people do. Y'all were at the meeting the other night. You saw how folks behaved. Last thing I need is all kinds of trouble in this town."

"So does that mean you've made up your mind?" my father asked.

"Did I say that?" the police chief replied.

Daddy kept on. "When will you decide?"

Mr. Monroe glanced at a calendar on the wall. "I'm thinking to announce it by the fifth of July."

My daddy looked disappointed. "That's three weeks away. I thought you needed help for the parade. You told me yourself you were shorthanded."

Whoosh ping! "Don't talk to me about the parade. We might not even have one this year, what with all this going on."

I gasped. No parade? The lid rattled under my feet. I steadied myself against the brick.

Mr. Monroe scraped back his chair. "Dang alleycats," he grumbled. "Drive me crazy in them cans all day."

Hearing him plod to the window, I shrank below the sill, certain my goose was cooked. "Scat, you varmints! Git!" he hollered down the alley. Then he perched on the window's edge, his butt hanging just above my head.

I heard my father say, "Elmo, don't wait that long to decide. You're asking for trouble."

"Then how about I say no right now?" Mr. Monroe growled. And turning his head, he hocked his wad right out the window. It sailed dripping past my face, inches away.

Next thing I knew, the lid I was standing on shot up and dropped me yelping into the can. It toppled over, making a tremendous racket, and left me sprawled half in, half out.

"What in tarnation—?" the police chief roared.

I scrunched in the can like a crab in its shell. Inside it was damp and sticky, with that sickly sour garbage smell.

After what seemed like an eternity, my father said, "Audrey Ina."

"Yes, sir?" The words rolled around the can and through my scrambled brain.

"Come out of there. Now."

"Yes, sir." I crawled out. My pedal pushers were torn, my knee was scraped, and I stunk to high heaven.

My father and Mr. Monroe stood at the window. Daddy's brows were so drawn, I feared they'd slid down his nose. "Audrey Ina, what do you think you're doing?"

"Daddy, I was worried about you."

"That's no excuse!" he thundered. "Gentlemen, I apologize for my inquisitive daughter." He frowned at me. "What am I going to do with you?"

"I shudder to think."

The police chief scratched his cheek. "I could lock her up, Nat."

My father sighed. "It's a thought. Audrey, go inside and wait for me. And keep in mind, you're in serious trouble."

"Yes, sir."

I limped up the stairs past the front desk. Frances's eyes widened as I plunked down on the bench opposite her.

"Whew," she whispered across the room. "You stink."

"I fell in the garbage—"

She held up a hand. "Don't tell me, don't even tell me. I don't want to know."

I leaned my head against the wall. There was no way to guess how Daddy would punish me for spying on him like that.

I closed my eyes. My father might want to believe that everything was going to work out, but I was not convinced. Far as I could tell, Mr. Monroe had no intention of hiring Mr. Cardwell. And I couldn't help wishing he would just say so now.

8

Turned out my punishment for sneaking off and snooping was that I was confined to the yard for two whole weeks, unless I was with an adult. That did not surprise me.

What *did* surprise me was seeing my picture on the front page of the *Advance* the next morning! It showed me on the station steps with Daddy and Mr. Cardwell, startled looks across all our faces. Much as they'd tried to keep the meeting secret, someone had snapped our picture as we left. Under the photo was the caption: "Councilman Nathan Stern and daughter Audrey accompany Lovelle Cardwell to police station." That wasn't exactly accurate, but I was in no position to argue.

The headline read: COLORED MAN PURSUES JOB ON POLICE FORCE. That surprised me too. Hadn't Sam said the *Advance* didn't give importance to Negro news? The article reported that Police Chief Monroe would announce his decision on July 5, the day after the parade. Looked like he'd gotten his way.

Seeing my face in the paper gave me a jolt. And it didn't help one bit when June said they might as well have put it on a billboard in downtown Blue Gap. I'd run into her at the five-and-dime that afternoon. After much persuasion, my mother had agreed to let me join her shopping, so long as I stuck to her like glue.

June was tickled pink about my picture. "And on the front page too! Only you looked like something the cat drug in."

So while Momma dawdled over the lipsticks, I told my friend the whole story of yesterday, including the part about falling in the garbage can. "You trashy thing," she remarked when I was done.

We looked at each other and busted out laughing. We giggled so long and hard, we drew stares from the blue-haired saleswoman and had to run to the ladies' room to pull ourselves together.

June splashed cold water on her face. "My father doesn't think Mr. Monroe will hire Mr. Cardwell."

"Neither do I."

She pulled on the cloth towel dispenser. "He said they only put y'all's picture in the paper to make trouble for your daddy."

I frowned. "What else did he say?"

"He said the editor of the paper doesn't just hate Negroes, he hates us Jews too. So it probably gave him no end of satisfaction to let the world know your daddy's trying to help colored folks better themselves."

"I don't see what's the big deal." I leaned down to sip from the spigot, not wanting her to see how her words got to me.

Back in the store, I looked around for Momma. June nudged me with her elbow. "There's that Edwina Clark," she whispered. Edwina was going through fabrics in the sewing aisle.

"Oh, who cares?" I put my nose skyward and in a voice that carried told June to come on.

Edwina didn't hardly glance up as we slid by. "Guess you don't say hey, now that you're famous."

"Guess not," I called back, happy to oblige.

"Of course I wouldn't be caught dead on the front page for helping a nigger."

June looked startled by Edwina's rudeness. "Don't pay her any mind, June," I said.

"Be too bad if the parade got canceled though," Edwina let fly.

I groaned. Dr. Einstein was wrong. Light wasn't the swiftest thing in the universe: Gossip was.

June turned to Edwina. "What are you talking about?"

"I like this calico, don't you?" Edwina remarked, ignoring her question. "Mother's making me a costume for the parade, no matter what. I'm supposed to ride on the float for the Daughters of the American Revolution this year."

The Daughters of the American Revolution was a club for highfalutin' white Gentile ladies. Needless to say, neither my mother nor June's had ever been invited to join.

"Oh, I think I'll just lay down right here and die of envy," I said, putting my hand to my forehead.

"It's not my fault y'all can't ride on it."

"Well, don't get your hopes up, Edwina. Like you said, we might not even have the parade."

"Maybe we won't, Audrey Stern."

"Serve you right," I muttered.

"Would someone please tell me what y'all are talking about?" June insisted.

"Guess you haven't heard, June." Edwina sighed. "Be a shame, wouldn't it?"

"Be worse than a shame," answered June. "It'd be criminal."

Edwina's smile was snide. "Tell Audrey's daddy that." She took June by the arm. "I heard it with my own ears. My cousin Homer told my mother he heard Mr. Monroe say that if things got too out of hand, he would cancel the parade, one-two-three. And with Audrey's father pushing that nigger to be on the police force, I guess folks are just bound to be upset with Mr. Stern."

"Upset how?" fretted June.

"I'm sure I don't know." Edwina's eyes were on me. "But I'd hate to have that on my head, wouldn't you? I would hate to go back to school in September being the one whose daddy ruined the parade."

Just then a welcome voice said, "Here you are." It was Momma, sounding relieved, till she saw my face. "What's wrong?"

I shrugged. "Nothing."

"Edwina said it'd be Mr. Stern's fault if the parade got canceled," June volunteered in a tiny voice.

"Oh, she did?" My mother took in Edwina for the first time.

Edwina shrank some. "I was just repeating what I heard."

"Well, maybe you ought not," Momma told her. "Rumors can be hurtful. 'Love thy neighbor.' Isn't that what Jesus said?"

"How do you know what Jesus said?" Edwina asked, staring.

My mother put on the blinking smile she reserved for idiots. "Edwina, I can read."

Red blotches appeared on Edwina's cheeks. She turned and walked away.

Momma put an arm around our shoulders. "Come on, girls. Let's get us some ice cream. I'm in need of something sweet."

Uncle Lewis came to supper that evening, same as he did every Tuesday. He picked up Tante at Marylou's Millinery on Main Street, where she worked making dresses and trimming hats, and drove her home.

Dinner was dismal. Nobody said a word about the article or the photo. Uncle Lewis droned on about molars and root canals, and every now and then Momma said, "Isn't that interesting?" just to be polite.

When the phone rang, I jumped up, glad for an excuse, and ran to the hall to get it. "Hello?"

A man's voice rasped in my ear. "This the Stern place?"

"Y-yes, sir," I stammered.

"I got a message for your daddy." I waited, heart pounding. "You tell him I said '*Heil* Hitler.'" Then the phone clicked off in my ear.

"Who is it, honey?" Momma called.

I walked back in. "They had a message for Daddy."

Everybody turned. "What'd they say?" my father asked. I hesitated, full of dread. "Audrey?"

"They said—'Heil Hitler.'"

The grown-ups bolted up. Looks of alarm zinged around the table. Tante's hands flew to her mouth.

"What's 'Heil Hitler'?"Joel asked.

Nobody answered. Daddy kept his gaze on me. "Audrey Ina, come here." I went into the crook of his arm. "Just tell me, did you recognize the voice?"

"No, sir. It was a man though."

"Did he say anything else?"

"No, sir."

He squeezed me. "I'm sorry it was you who took the call. You best let Momma or me answer the phone from now on."

I crept to my seat, glancing at Tante. She sat stone still, staring at her hands.

The kitchen was dead quiet till Uncle Lewis' fist hit the table, making the dishes jump. "Now do you get it, Nathan?"

Eyes lowered, Tante began to rock. When she spoke, her voice had a dull, empty sound. "Every day I ask myself, why? Why did God spare me?"

Momma reached for Tante's hand. "Tante, it's all right—"

"Why did I not die with Mama and Gitel and the rest?" She raised her eyes to Daddy. "Is this why, Nathan? For more of Hitler's hate?"

"Tante, listen to me," Momma insisted. "There's no Hitler here. He's dead, he's gone."

"How can you say that, Selma?" she replied. "When he is with me all the time. He and that hell he made." I knew she meant Auschwitz.

"I can smell the bodies burning," she whispered. "I have ashes in my mouth."

The words spilled onto the table, full of horror. Momma closed her eyes.

"Tante." My father sounded miserable. "Forgive me."

In answer she began to cry, her sobs a fist around my heart. We sat like that until her tears slowly ebbed. Dusty beams of sun fell across our cold food.

At last she got up. "I think I will go to my room now."

Momma reached for her hand again. "Will you be all right?"

She pulled away. "No." Then she went down, taking all the air in the kitchen with her.

A dry wind was gusting when I slipped into the yard that night. It scudded along the grass, making a sound like footsteps. I shone the flashlight into the blackness. How icy and distant the stars were. Their light had to journey for years and years across the emptiness of space. And what I was seeing now was how they'd looked when that light first left them, all that time ago. I might be sitting in the present, but when I gazed at the night sky, I was peering back into the past.

That was how Tante had been at the supper table. It might have appeared like she was here with us, but the truth was, she was somewhere else—back in her dark and terrifying past.

It was the first time I'd heard her talk like that about the war, and it had taken the phone call to make it leak out. What had happened to her family and everyone she knew? And they were only a handful of the six million Jews who had died. I'd heard that number before, but it had always been that—a number. Now the enormity of it hit me.

The night was flung with stars. Six thousand, the astronomy book said, that you could actually see with the naked eye. If you took six thousand and multiplied it one thousand times, that gave you six million. Six million people killed—

It was too much to think about. I rose to go inside, when a movement in the laundry room caught my eye.

I crept to the window. Tante stood at the sink, pale as a ghost in the shadows. Hot water poured from the faucet as she dug at her tattoo with a washcloth, whispering in Polish.

I stepped away, afraid she'd notice me standing above her. But my aunt was like someone lost in a dream. I could see the numbers on her arm, raw where the washcloth worried them. Hard as she tried, they would not wash away.

All at once the shadows seemed to shift and I no longer saw Tante there, but a young girl—head shaved, painfully thin, tearing at her scarred skin. She lifted her face and I looked into her lost gray eyes—

I stumbled back; the girl vanished. In her place was Tante again, holding her arm. She turned off the water and drifted back to her room.

I sank into the grass. Above me swirled the galaxy, a giant pinwheel of stars. In the vast night Tante's past beckoned, and a young girl called to me from a place not so far away.

9

The smell of homemade biscuits woke me the next morning. The grown-ups were already at table when I came down, passing the marmalade and avoiding one another's eyes.

Momma pulled a pan from the oven. "Hello, sleepy-head," she said. "Look, I made your favorite." She held out a cheek for me to kiss; for once her cheeriness seemed strained.

I stole a glance at Tante. She was squeezing a grape-fruit and reading the morning news.

"Come eat," Momma told me.

"I'm still asleep." I yawned and went out on the porch. Joel sat on the steps, feeding crumbs to a shoe box of tiny striped worms. "What're those, Brother?"

"Callerpittars." He raised his eyes to mine. "Tante says they grow up to be butterflies."

"Gee, wish I could do that."

I settled in the swing. The day was already hot. Even the robins were quiet, preferring the cool of dawn for pulling up earthworms. Heat waves shimmied off the driveway where the Studebaker sat, a lopsided heap on four flat tires.

"Daddy." I tried to keep my voice steady. "You best come here."

"What is it?" He hurried out, napkin tucked in his

belt. I pointed to the car. "Oh, my God," he said.

Momma and Tante came out then and all of us went over to the car. Each tire had been slashed once.

I felt sick. I was in the yard late last night. To my recollection, the car had been fine then. This must have happened after I went in.

My daddy pulled the napkin from his belt. "I'm calling Mr. Monroe," he declared, and went into the house.

Tante put a cigarette to her mouth. She fumbled with the matches till Momma took them from her and struck one. My aunt held the cigarette to the flame, blowing out a ragged spiral of smoke.

"I can't believe someone actually came in our yard," I ventured. Momma shot me a look that told me to hush.

"Believe it." Tante brushed ashes off her skirt. "If someone wants to harm you, they will stop at nothing. They will come in your house, if they want to."

"No one is coming into our house, Audrey." Momma spoke to me, but her words were for Tante. "We have laws here to protect us."

My aunt snorted. "Don't be foolish, Selma. How many warnings do you need?"

"Tante, please—" Momma said.

"What?" she scoffed. "You think I don't know what I am talking about? I know. We had warnings too. There were signs."

"In Poland, do you mean?" I asked.

"Audrey," Momma cautioned.

"Momma, I'm just asking. What kinds of signs, Tante?"

"Just—signs," she replied.

I watched the ash grow on the end of her still cigarette. Then suddenly she began to speak, as if her voice had been unfastened. "I remember we are making bread. For Rosh Hashanah. Mama and Gitel and me. Even though we have heard—that Hitler's soldiers are coming closer—"

Her words tumbled out in broken spurts, like water in a spigot that'd been turned off too long. "And then they are there. In the cottage."

I imagined soldiers wearing the Nazi emblem, the spidery black swastika, storming into her house. She surprised me by saying, "Three women. I never see them before. They are not from Jarzyna. They walk in. No knock, no greeting. One of them grabs Mama's pot for making soup. Another takes the little hand mill for grinding grain that was my grandmama's. And Mama is yelling at them, 'Thieves! Get out of my house!'

"I grab the broom. I am always the hotheaded one. Not like Gitel—"

She faltered, her face washed with sudden grief. "I think I can beat those three witches out of the house by myself. But one takes the broom from behind me. And the other slaps me in the face until I am seeing stars. They take the broom. They take everything. One sees the ribbon in Gitel's hair and rips that from her too. 'Where you Jews are going,' she tells us, 'you won't be needing this.' And then they are gone."

In the hush that followed, the tip of Tante's cigarette glowed. "A month later," she said, matter-of-factly now, "the Nazis come to Jarzyna. They round us up and take us in their trucks to the ghetto."

*　*　*

Momma and I stood in the yard long after Tante's story had ended. My aunt went and lay in the hammock, staring up into the sweet gum. Finally Momma said, "Come on," and she and I went in to clear the breakfast dishes.

Inside Daddy told us, "Frances won't be coming in today. The Cardwells' tires were slashed too."

After a while Mr. Monroe pulled up in his white patrol car. Daddy went out to greet him, Momma and me right behind. The police chief frowned at the Studebaker and spit in my mother's azaleas. He lifted his hat. "Mrs. Stern."

Tante had gotten up from the hammock. My father waved her over. "Elmo, I believe you know my aunt."

Her face hardened; anyone in uniform made her wary. Mr. Monroe rubbed the back of his neck. "We've howdied, but we ain't shook." He held out his big paw. "Miss Minkowitch," he said with unusual mildness. She pumped the tips of his fingers twice.

"And of course you know my daughter, Audrey," Daddy said drylike.

I felt my cheeks burn. The police chief grunted. "If y'all don't mind, I'd like to get down to brass tacks." He pulled a smudged notepad from his pocket, dabbed a pencil on his tongue. "You got any idea what time the incident took place?"

Before anyone could answer, Uncle Lewis's Ford swerved up to the curb. My uncle jumped out, bow tie askew. "Damn you, Nathan!" he shouted.

"Lewis," cried Momma. "For God's sake, what's wrong?"

His face was ashen. "Someone painted a swastika on the shul."

Things happened fast after that. Mr. Monroe slapped his hat against his leg. Then he and Daddy slammed into the patrol car and off they roared. Inside the phone began to ring. Momma rushed to get it. "Audrey, keep an eye on Brother, will you?"

I ran after her. "Okay, but Momma? Can Uncle Lewis take me by the shul? Please, Momma, please."

She picked up the phone. "Hello?"

"I'll come straight back this time, I promise."

Momma wrapped a hand over the receiver. "Audrey, quit pestering me. It's the rabbi calling."

I whirled out to where Uncle Lewis was saying to Tante, "Do you want to go to work? I can drive you."

She nodded numbly. "I get my purse," she said, and went into the house. My uncle thrust his hands in his pockets and paced the backyard.

I crouched beside Joel. "Brother," I whispered. "Don't move from here, okay?"

He blinked. "Okay."

"I'll be back in two shakes of a lamb's tail. So don't go anywhere. Promise?"

"Promise," he whispered.

I snuck around to the street side of my uncle's car. Hoisting myself up, I slithered in the back window. I didn't dare risk slamming the door shut.

The backseat was strewn with newspapers, which I made into a pillow of sorts, hunkering down on the floor behind the driver's seat. Here I was, going off again without telling, knowing full well I'd pay for it later. I didn't care.

At last Uncle Lewis and Tante got in the car; it screeched away from the curb. Their heads shone faintly in the back windshield as Blue Gap rolled past—tree by tree, pole by pole—backwards.

Uncle Lewis lurched onto Langhorne Road. "Do you—want to—see the shul?" he stammered.

Tante shrugged in answer. She flicked her cigarette out the window. "Poor Nathan," I heard her murmur.

"Poor *Nathan*?" my uncle echoed in disbelief.

She tilted her head. "I surprise you, Lewis. I tell you why I say this. He is so like my tata. Also blind, also foolish. Tata could not believe anyone was so evil as Hitler."

"Maybe he needed to think that to—" My uncle stopped himself.

She finished his thought. "To what? To survive? It did not help him survive, did it?"

I turned my head to catch every word. My aunt had been silent about the war for so long. Now it seemed the events of last night and this morning were prying her memory open and she could no longer contain the flood of thoughts and feelings inside her.

Her voice turned bitter. "Even in the ghetto, where they squeeze us in with the rats and the lice, Tata is saying it could be worse. When we are so hungry, we are crying from this hunger, still he says this. And I am thinking, what could be worse?"

She lowered her voice. "Then we go to Auschwitz and I find out."

They didn't speak again till the car stopped in front of Marylou's. Uncle Lewis turned to her. "Tante, I—I don't know what to say."

"Say good-bye. What else can you say?" She got out and slammed the door.

My uncle drove down Main Street, parked in front of his office, and went up. The heat swam over me as I stumbled onto the sidewalk and ran the three blocks to the synagogue.

Closer to shul I slowed, in case Daddy and Mr. Monroe were around. But there was no sign of the patrol car. Instead I saw a crowd gathered in front.

I wasn't about to have come all that way for nothing, so I went and hid behind a mailbox. There was the swastika, smeared on the white door, sinister and black.

The sun glared down. It was one thing to see a picture of it in a history book, another to have it flung on a place that was sacred, a place you thought of as yours. I imagined Nazi soldiers with thick boots and cruel faces. The people standing here were workaday folks—farmers in overalls, housewives in hats. Miss Farley was there, windblown as ever. And so was Edwina, holding her mother's gloved hand; they wore twin smirks.

The door to the synagogue opened and Rabbi Grody came out, carrying a pail of whitewash. Muscular and sturdy, he had on blue suspenders and a black skullcap; under his arms, his shirt was soaked through.

Miss Farley stepped from the crowd. "Rabbi." Her voice was quaking. "I want to say that I think this is an outrage. I could die of shame for all of us today."

"Thank you, Henrietta," the rabbi replied. "I appreciate it." She turned then and whipped up the street, taking her tiny storm with her.

Nobody else said a word. Rabbi Grody crouched and stirred the paint. He laid a thin white stroke on the door, but the black still showed. Stepping back, he pulled out a handkerchief and mopped his forehead.

"Gracious," I heard Mrs. Clark whisper. "He's sweating like a pig."

"Hope he don't get paint on his marmaduke," a familiar voice said, making me duck back behind the mailbox. It was Buster LaCoste; his pimple-faced friend was with him.

The Rabbi eyed Buster. "It's called a *yarmulke*."

"I beg your pardon," the boy answered, not a bit of sorry in it.

The pimply kid cuffed Buster. "Shut up, you idiot. Can't you see the man's trying to work?"

Buster squatted at the curb, frowning. The other boy sauntered to the door. "Going to take three or four coats," he said, putting a finger through the new paint.

Rabbi Grody pretended not to notice. "I believe you're right."

"Too hot for it," the boy went on, enjoying himself.

Right then I wished the ground would open up and swallow me, it hurt so much to see the rabbi standing there, taking those boys' sass.

"You ought to leave it," Buster suggested, fingers sifting a handful of dirt.

Rabbi Grody dipped the brush again. "No, I don't think I will."

The pimple-faced boy looked at Buster. "Yeah, might just have to wash it off again tomorrow."

Buster snickered. "Waste of good whitewash, if you

ask me." And he tossed some dirt right into the pail.

"Hey!" I shouted. I didn't stop to think; I ran forward.

The crowd buzzed. "Audrey, what are you doing here?" the Rabbi demanded.

"I just come by." I hardly knew what I was saying, my heart was bouncing fit to be tied. "Want me to give you a hand, Rabbi? I'm real good. I helped my daddy paint the toolshed—" I trailed off, wishing I hadn't mentioned my daddy.

Buster peered into the pail at the ruined whitewash. "Aw, Red, look what you made me do."

"Wasn't me, it was you," I returned.

"Are you calling me a liar?"

Rabbi Grody got between us. "That's enough."

"Everybody saw you do it," I told Buster, turning to the crowd. Their stares back were cold and ugly. Edwina had gloat in her eyes.

"Go home, Audrey," the rabbi cautioned.

"No." I eyed the crowd. "I'll go when they go."

"Oh!" Mrs. Clark cried. "Someone needs to take a belt to that child."

"Me?" I told her. "It's y'all who ought to be ashamed of yourselves."

"Audrey," the rabbi urged. "Go."

"Yeah," a man grumbled. "And tell your Jew daddy to mind his own damn business."

I stamped my foot. "Don't you talk about my father like that."

"Well, no nigger cop is giving me a parking ticket," another yelled.

"Park that Jew right in the river," the pimply boy sneered.

The crowd hooted. Hot tears stung my eyes. "Shut up, just shut up, you—Nazis!" I cried. Then my feet twirled me around and I peeled off up Main Street.

10

"In the history section today, Audrey?" Miss Farley asked in the library, minutes later. "I'm used to seeing you in science, wayfaring the cosmos."

"Yes, ma'am, Miss Farley, hey." I glued my eyes to the shelves and prayed she wouldn't notice how flushed I was.

I knew Momma would be worried sick about me by now, but I'd ducked into the library hoping to find something that would help me make sense of what I'd just seen, something to make me feel safe again.

"Searching for anything in particular?"

I hesitated. "I'm looking for stuff about the Nazis, if you must know."

"Audrey." She turned me to her. "You saw the swastika, didn't you?"

"Oh, Miss Farley," I burst out. "I hate them!"

She sighed. "You hate them, they hate you. And where does that get us?"

"I don't care, they deserve it!"

"Hush, dear, or I'll have to act like a librarian and ask you to leave." She herded me to a chair and sat down beside me.

"What is wrong with people anyhow?" I asked, wiping my face on my arm.

She shook her head. "How's your aunt taking it?"

"It's brought up some awfully bad memories in her."
I turned back to the shelves. "Miss Farley, have you got
any books about Auschwitz?"

"Audrey, I don't think you want to get into all that—"

"But you're the one who said we ought not to forget
these things."

Miss Farley opened her mouth and closed it. From the
shelf on World War II, she pulled out three large volumes
and loaded them into my arms. "There, that ought to get
you going."

I carried the books to a table by the window. Sunlight
filtered through the blinds; the traffic rumbled pleasantly
by. Outside, it was Blue Gap as usual.

The first book I opened told how Adolf Hitler had considered the Jews to be a separate race of people. In 1935
he'd passed something called the Nuremberg Laws,
which were meant to keep Jews apart from the rest of the
German people. They sounded a lot like our own segregation laws.

In September of 1939, the year after Kristallnacht,
the Nazis had invaded Poland and that was what started
the war. There was a picture of a ghetto in the Polish city
of Lublin, a grainy photo of Jewish kids with yellow stars
sewn on their ragged clothes. They sat on a curb near the
bodies of people who had perished of hunger in the
street.

In another book I read how Hitler was determined to
destroy everyone in Europe who was not Aryan. Aryans
were white Gentiles. If a person had any Jewish blood in
them at all, he did not consider them Aryan.

A photograph from the Warsaw ghetto showed Jews

being rounded up to be sent to a death camp called Treblinka. The Gestapo had dragged them from their houses and was forcing them down the street; behind them the ghetto was in flames. The captives marched, carrying their few belongings, fear and despair on their faces.

There was a picture of the trains too, the hot, crowded cattle cars that had carried the Jews to the camps. No doubt Tante had ridden in one of those.

A feeling for my aunt washed over me then, sharp and sad, tinged with shame. How could I ever have felt anything but pity for her?

Miss Farley rested a hand on my shoulder. "How you coming?"

I asked her to explain why Hitler had wanted only Aryans in his country. She thought a moment. "Hitler's mind was very twisted, Audrey. He had a sick idea of what a perfect world should be."

She went on to say how the Nazis had persecuted the black-eyed Gypsies and the dark Slavic people too. And there was no place in Hitler's world for the elderly, the feebleminded, or the crippled. By the end of the war, eight million people had been slaughtered by Nazi hands.

"*Eight* million?" I asked. "So it wasn't only Jews."

"Oh, the Jews got the brunt of it, Audrey, no doubt about it. But in Hitler's perfect world there would only be people who were young and healthy and Aryan."

I thought about that. "Miss Farley? Do you think the person who painted the swastika on the synagogue really knew what they were doing?"

"No, I don't. But that doesn't make it any less

dangerous, now does it?" She squeezed my shoulder and was gone.

I stared at a picture of Hitler, with his weakish face and mad watery eyes. Next to it was a photo of prisoners behind a barbed-wire fence; in the background were rows of stark barracks. The caption read: "Jewish inmates at Osweicm." Osweicm was the Polish town where a death camp had been built; the Nazis had renamed it Auschwitz.

The prisoners' uniforms hung on their starved bodies, and, like the young Tante I'd glimpsed in the laundry room, their shaved heads held dead, empty eyes. The book said they carried out the work of the camp.

Then it gave a description of what had happened to most of the Jews and other prisoners once they arrived, as told by someone who'd actually been there. This was what I read:

> A German writer, visiting the Nazi death camp at Auschwitz, Poland, in 1943, issued the following report:
>
> Beyond the barracks is a small plain building labeled "Showers." In actuality, it is a gas chamber.
>
> Jewish prisoners, arriving on trains from the ghettoes, are put in two lines. One—made up of those with any strength left—is for workers for the camp. The other—mostly women, children, the sick, and the old—is sent to the "Showers."
>
> Those chosen for extermination are stripped of their clothes. Then they are driven into the building with shouts, kicks, and whips, packed in hundreds at a time.

The doors are closed and sealed. A cry goes up as deadly gas pours from the showerheads. All die within fifteen minutes.

The gas is pumped out. The doors are opened. Other prisoners remove the bodies and take them to the crematoriums to be burned. The huge ovens are fired night and day. Ashes rain down from the tall chimneys, leaving a stench in the air that can be smelled for miles.

I slammed the book shut and fled to the lavatory. Locking the door behind me, I put my face in the sink and let the cold water run over it, until I couldn't tell what was water and what were tears.

I left the library without saying good-bye to Miss Farley. She'd been so kind to me, but all I wanted now was to get home to Momma.

Heading down Westerly Drive, I saw her on the porch, a hand shading her eyes. "You scared me to death, Audrey Ina," she yelled as I came up the walk.

She looked shaken. "You deliberately disobeyed by leaving the yard. And you left your brother alone."

She swatted me once, hard, on my behind. I busted out crying. She took hold of my shoulders. "Where have you been? Whatever possessed you to run off like that again?"

I covered my face. "I'm sorry."

"Are you?"

"More than you know."

She seemed alarmed. "Audrey, what happened?"

"Oh, Momma," I cried and went into her arms.

She held me. Then, sitting me down on the swing, she pulled a crumpled tissue from her pocket. I took it and, wiping away my tears, I commenced to tell her everything. I even confessed to seeing Tante in the laundry room the night before. All the while, Momma said nothing. Her eyes grew troubled when I described the swastika, and her jaw fairly dropped when I told about trying to help the rabbi. When I'd finished, she said, "Honestly, Audrey, half the time I don't know whether to spank you or hug you."

"You already spanked me," I reminded her.

She put her arms around me. "I guess a hug's in order then."

"I only made things worse at shul, Momma." My voice shook. "They said disgusting things about Daddy."

"But you tried to help, honey, that's what matters."

Then I told her about what I'd learned at the library. She brushed my bangs off my forehead. "I was kind of hoping you could stay a kid a little longer. I guess that's not possible now."

"Oh, Momma." Tears welled up again. "How could people let anybody do such cruel things?"

She sighed. "Hard as it is to believe, Audrey, there were lots of people who agreed with Hitler. There's been a long history of prejudice against Jews in Europe."

"Is that why Grandma Lena left?"

"Uh-huh."

"Why didn't Tante's family?"

"I think sometimes it's difficult for people to leave their home. No matter how bad things get, it's still home.

"Even before Hitler," she went on, "there was terrible violence against the Jews. Great storms of persecution called pogroms, where thousands of Jews were tortured and killed."

"Why? What did they do to deserve that?"

"Nothing, honey. They were scapegoats."

"They were what?" I'd never heard that expression before.

"A scapegoat is someone who gets blamed for someone else's mistakes," she explained. "I guess it's easier to blame someone else, than to try and fix what's wrong yourself."

"Is it kind of like when Tante hurts my feelings and then for no reason I get mad at Joel?"

Momma smiled. "It's exactly like that." She grew serious. "You'll have to be punished for running off. Audrey, promise me you won't go rushing headlong into things you know nothing about."

"I think I've learned my lesson, Momma."

"I hope so. And no more going out in the yard at night, hear?"

"Yes, ma'am." The image of young Tante rose before me. "Momma? Why did they tattoo her?"

"I think they wanted her to feel like she was less than a person. So they took away her name and made her a number instead.

"They took everything. Her home, her family, her name—"

Momma hesitated. "Audrey? Want to see a picture of Tante's family?"

"Really?"

She motioned me to follow her inside. Joel slept, sprawled out in front of the TV, his shoe box of caterpillars close by. Momma put a finger to her lips and we went up to her room.

There she spilled the contents of her jewelry box out on her bed. From under bracelets, earrings, and pins, she drew a fold of white tissue paper. Careful fingers lifted the paper to reveal a faded brown photograph.

In it a man, woman, and two young girls sat under a tree in a windswept meadow. They wore simple, well-made clothing and smiled at the camera with looks of shy wonderment.

"Was this in Jarzyna?" I asked.

"Uh-huh."

Tante's tata was tall, with thick glasses and an impish grin. "He was a musician," Momma told me. "And her mother was a seamstress."

"Like Tante is now."

Dark and pretty, her mother held an armful of wildflowers. She had her head tilted at the camera in a teasing sort of way. And there was Gitel, a ribbon tying back blond hair, framing a sweet face. "She kind of looks like you, Momma," I said, touching the image.

"You think so? And who does Tante look like, I wonder?"

Though two years younger, Pesel was almost as big as her sister, her eyes liquid. But it was her hair that gave me pause. Thick with curls, something made me certain it was red—"

"Momma," I practically shouted. "She has my hair."

"You have her hair," she corrected me.

"Only what happened to it? It's not like that now."

"It never grew back the same. Not after Auschwitz. Poor Pesel—" Momma's voice broke. "They even took her hair."

I gazed at the faces of my aunt's family. All that remained of them was this fading piece of paper and Tante's memories.

My mother was crying. I leaned against her. "Sorry," she sniffed, and kissed my shoulder.

"Momma?" I asked softlike. "What did Tante do in the camp? Do you know?"

"Believe it or not, Audrey," she answered, wiping her eyes, "I think she sewed. I think someone found out she could sew and put her to work mending the uniforms of the Nazis who ran the camp."

"She must have been so lonely."

"So lonely." Momma took the picture from me and began wrapping it back up.

"Where'd you get the photo anyhow?"

"Grandma Lena gave it to me. Years ago, before the war. She wanted me to know my Polish cousins." She held it out to me. "Here, Audrey, I want you to have it now."

I took it from her. "Thank you, Momma, I'll cherish it. Only shouldn't it be Tante's?"

"I tried to give it to her, honey, when she first came here. She couldn't look at it, she said it would hurt too much. She hasn't mentioned it since."

11

Frances came back to work early the next morning. Soon as I saw her limping up the walk, I knew things had gone from bad to worse. The air was thick as bathwater as I ran out to meet her. "Frances, what's wrong?"

She hobbled past without answering. I dogged her into the kitchen, where she sat, pulling off her shoes. Her feet were rubbed raw and bloody. "Fetch me a damp cloth, child," she said.

"Don't keep me in suspense," I told her, bringing a rag.

She dabbed at her toes, wincing. "That dang driver wouldn't let me on the bus. So I walked."

"From Fifth Street? That's practically four miles!"

"Don't tell me."

Turned out Frances had set out for work in the early dark, intending to make up for yesterday. The light was just breaking through the haze as the bus pulled to her stop. Only when the driver saw who it was waiting, he said, "Won't have no uppity niggers on my bus," and shut the door in her face.

"I swear steam start to come out my ears," Frances huffed. "I guess I could have took my chances and waited for the next one. Except I was so ticked, I just started walking."

"Goodness," I breathed. "Things are going to hell in a handbasket."

"What kind of talk is that?" She took my hand. "I'm just heartsick about your shul, Audrey Ina." Her eyes shifted toward the basement. "How's Miss Minkowitz?"

"Not good," I replied. "We haven't seen her at all since she came home from work yesterday."

Frances shook her head. Upstairs we could hear Daddy padding into the bathroom. "Run get me my flops," she whispered. I brought her the old cotton slippers she wore about the house.

She tied on her apron. "Don't breathe a word of this to Mr. Stern, hear? I expect he's got enough to worry about."

Daddy came down soon after, patches of shaving cream clinging to his chin. "Morning, Frances," he said. "Everything all right?"

My daddy was running ragged. It was way past midnight when I heard him come in last night. He and the rabbi had kept a watch at the shul.

"Right as can be." Frances held out a steaming cup of coffee. "Mr. Cardwell says thank you for sending the tow truck for the car."

But my father was frowning down at her feet. Red stained the white cloth of her slippers front and back. "What's this?" he asked.

Frances fanned a hand. "Oh, just my corns acting up."

"Since when do you have corns on your heels?" His eyes went from her to me and back again. "Frances?"

So while I ran to get the gauze to bind her blisters,

she described her morning to him. Daddy was swiping his chin when I returned. "I'm reporting that driver," he declared.

"Don't you do it, Mr. Stern," Frances protested. "I wasn't going to tell you this either, but the reverend got himself a nasty phone call last night."

My daddy sighed. "I'm sorry to hear that."

"All I'm saying is, things are heating up in this town. I can't bear for y'all to have more trouble than you already do."

"Frances, Elmo needs to know about this," my father insisted.

"I suspect he'll hear about it without you telling him," I chimed in.

Daddy put down his cup. "Well, you're probably right about that, Audrey. I'll bet he gets an earful too."

"You sound like you feel sorry for him."

"Frankly, honey, we've put Mr. Monroe in a tough position. After all, the decision to hire Mr. Cardwell does ultimately rest with him."

"He ought to do what's right and not worry about what people think," I declared.

"Absolutely," Daddy agreed. "But Elmo Monroe is a prudent man. And how the citizens of Blue Gap behave is going to influence his decision."

"Well, I hope he doesn't do anything rash. Like cancel the parade. I shudder to think how folks'd behave then."

Daddy threw up his hands. "All right, you win. I'll keep my mouth shut this one time. But you're not walking to work again, Frances. I'll drive you home myself tonight."

"No need, Mr. Stern," she replied. "That driver's only on the morning run. They aren't all that way."

"You can use my bike," I offered her. "I'm not riding it much these days."

Daddy gave me a severe look. "You won't be riding it at all, Audrey Ina. Not for the rest of the summer. That's your punishment for running off yesterday."

I hung my head. "Yes, sir."

He lifted my chin. "The rabbi told me what happened at shul." His gaze softened. "It's hard to be mad at a kid like you." And he gave me a quick smile before going back up.

Pretty soon Tante's footsteps sounded on the stairs. She came in, dressed for work in her usual black attire, tensing at the sight of Frances.

Frances wiped her hands on her apron. "Good morning, Miss Minkowitz," she said like always. "What can I get you?"

In answer my aunt went to the refrigerator and got out a grapefruit. We watched as she put two slices of bread in the toaster herself. Then, ignoring the fact that she was being ignored, Frances lit the water for Tante's coffee.

My aunt busied herself slicing the grapefruit. When the toast popped up, she gasped, jumpy as a cat. Frances reached out, ready. "Let me help you now."

Tante held up a hand. "I can do for myself, thank you very much." Her voice was brittle.

A trickle of blood ran from her finger. "Tante, you cut yourself," I heard myself say.

She examined the nick, shrugging. "What do you know? I can still bleed."

"You best wrap that up, Miss Minkowitz." Pulling some gauze from a drawer, Frances took a step toward her.

"Do not touch me." My aunt shrank away.

"Tante," I gasped.

"Audrey, hush." Frances's eyes never left my aunt. "Miss Minkowitz. You know I wouldn't harm you for the world."

My aunt grabbed a napkin, stuck her finger in it. "I do not want your help," she snapped. "Your help sticks in my throat."

Frances kept on in her same calm way. "I don't blame you for being angry. I'm angry too. But you got to understand something. We never asked Mr. Stern for his support. Everything he's done, he's done for his own good reasons—"

Tante slid her eyes at Frances and turned her face away.

"Mr. Cardwell tried to talk him out of it, that's God's honest truth." Frances's voice cracked. "Lord knows you're the last person on earth we'd want to see hurt—"

"What are you doing?" asked Joel from the doorway, making our heads turn. He held out the shoe box of caterpillars. "Look, Tante. They grew. Just like you said. They're two times bigger today."

"Let me see those, Joel." Frances waved him away from my aunt. She peered into the box, blinking. "Huh. Isn't that something?"

Brother nodded. "She's going to make me a cage for them, aren't you, Tante?"

Frances brushed his hair off his face. "And I know it'll be something beautiful."

My aunt covered her face with her hands. "Is Tante crying?" Brother asked Frances.

"No, child," she answered. "She's just tired. Why don't you take her out on the porch to rest?"

"Sure." He held up his hand and Tante let him lead her out.

Frances sat at the table, her arms across her waist. "Lord, Lord," she sighed. "That woman can break your heart."

"She acts like she's scared of you," I whispered.

"She's always been that way some. I think I was the first colored woman she ever knew."

"You'd think it'd be the opposite, wouldn't you? I mean, you'd think she'd feel friendly toward someone else who knows how hate feels."

"It don't work that way, child," Frances declared. "Your aunt's lived too long with way too much fear. She can't trust nobody." She smoothed her apron. "My Meemaw had those same eyes."

"Was she the one born into slavery?" I asked.

Frances had told me about her grandmother before. Meemaw was a little girl at the end of the Civil War when her family was finally freed. And though she lived to be ninety-four, Frances said she died a bitter old woman.

Gazing out the window, Frances said now, "I recall this one time—I couldn't have been more than four or five—Meemaw showed me where the man that had owned her had carved his initials onto her back."

"How awful."

"It was just a faded scar by then. But I won't ever forget what she told me. She said, 'They's carved on my heart too. And that never heals'."

Her hand made slow circles on the tablecloth. "I'll tell you one thing, Audrey Ina. I don't care how your aunt acts toward me. I got nothing but love for that woman. That woman's strong. She's a survivor."

That evening, while Tante napped in the hammock, I climbed up in the sweet gum above her. In the slanting light, her face was beautiful, a pale scar running through her brow.

Her arm was flung across her, causing a blue number to peek out from a loose cuff. I stared at it, wishing for a breeze to blow the sleeve farther back. When none came, I skinnied down, dangling while she brushed away a gnat. I inched over, twigs snapping underfoot. Soon I was beside her. My finger pushed back the cloth. There was the letter *J* followed by six numbers, etched on the white skin of her arm.

She grabbed my wrist. "What are you doing?"

"N-nothing, Tante." I tried to wriggle out of her grasp. "There was a bug on you."

Her fingers tightened. "Your nose will grow like Pinocchio."

My eyes were drawn again to the numbers. She covered them with her hand. "That must have hurt," I muttered.

Her eyes flashed steel. "You are wrong. I felt nothing."

"Really?"

The words burst out of her. "What would you feel if

the ashes of your family are floating in the air when they put this on you?"

I glanced at my own arm and for one second, I could almost see blue numbers across the freckled skin. "Tante?"

"What now?"

I wanted to tell her how brave I thought she was, and how I wished there was something I could do to comfort her. But when I looked at her closed face, the right words would not come.

"I'm sorry," I said. And she released my arm.

No one had to tell me it was wrong to go into Tante's room without her permission. It wouldn't have mattered anyway. I was being pulled along by something more powerful than curiosity.

Who was the real Pesel? Was she that impish girl in the photograph? Or the tortured young woman I thought of as my aunt? I figured the little doll under her bed, the one she'd called Pesel, might give me a clue.

The next afternoon found me on the steps outside her room, listening to the slap of Frances's iron in the laundry room. Finally I slipped inside and closed the door behind me.

All I could hear now was the hammering of my heart. From Tante's window I could see what she saw looking out: the backyard rolling into tall grass and fading into the hills.

Her bed jutted from the wall; on the night table beside it was a radio, clock, and ashtray. Books lay in a pile nearby, giving off a musty smell. The ones written in

Polish were filled with fascinating drawings and odd, curious words. I'd have been content to leaf through them all afternoon, but she'd be home sooner than later—and I had to be out before then.

My eyes swept the bare walls; the top of her bureau was empty too. Unlike Momma, Tante had no keepsakes of her family.

I crouched beside the bed and slid out the wooden box. The doll bumped inside. My fingers tingled with nervous excitement, till I realized the box was locked. I glanced around: Where would my aunt keep the key?

Creeping to her bureau, I pulled open the top drawer. The sight of her underwear gave me pause. Which was kind of ridiculous, if you thought about it. Here I was searching for my aunt's darkest secrets and I felt funny going through her slips.

One by one I rummaged the drawers. The bottom one was empty, save for some official-looking papers in Polish. I saw her name with the Polish spelling—Besel Minkowiecz, age 13—Jarzyna written beneath it, and her scrawled signature on the line below that. Her United States passport was dated April 1945; it had been issued after her release from Auschwitz. The picture shocked me: Here was the dead-eyed girl I'd seen in the laundry. Only the hair was different; bristly all over, it had started to grow again.

I laid the passport down and went to put the box back under the bed. That's when I noticed a drawer in the night table I must have missed before. Brushing my hand around inside it, my fingers moved over a tiny key.

I put it in the lock and turned; the clasp released. In

the hall Frances flew by and I froze till she went up into the kitchen. Tante's clock ticked furiously in my ear as I lifted up the lid.

Inside was the doll, about eight inches long, crudely fashioned from a broom handle, or maybe the leg of a chair. Stick arms pegged into the body moved up, down, and sideways. Big eyes and a lopsided grin had been notched into one end. Red thread was knotted through the top to look like hair.

I stared at that face; the face stared back. There was something so familiar about it, with its mischievous smile and red curls. The truth was it looked like Pesel. Hadn't my aunt smoothed the hair and called it by her name?

Ever so gently I turned it upside down. Letters had been carved into the bottom: *BM* above an *O. BM*, Tante's initials in Polish, told me what I'd already guessed: She had made the doll. But what did the *O* stand for?

I nearly dropped it then. Oscweicm! The Polish town where Auschwitz had been built. To think I was holding something that Tante had made there.

Only why had she made it? For company maybe, that I could understand. But how was it possible, since everything else had been taken away from her? And why had she kept it all these years, when it could only remind her of that terrible time?

I returned the box and the key to their hiding places. Then I crept back into the basement, leaving the little doll under her bed, just the way I'd found it.

12

An eyelash of a new moon hung over the shul when we arrived for services that Friday night. The twilight was still bright enough to see that the door held no trace of the swastika.

Inside folks stood in buzzing huddles. They went silent and parted to let us pass. Momma took my hand. "Hello, Shirley," she called to June's mother. Mrs. Silverman turned away.

We took our seats down front. The movie had started up next door; Woody Woodpecker's cackle pierced the walls. Uncle Lewis entered, saw us, and sat somewhere else.

I craned my neck to look for June. When she came in, I pulled on my ear, our signal to meet in the cloakroom.

We arrived the same time. I didn't bother with hello. "Jeepers, your mother gave us the cold shoulder."

June was practically in tears. "I can't come to your house any more."

"How come?"

"She doesn't want me anywhere near you. She thinks something dangerous might happen."

"Oh, June, your mother's a prodigious worrywart."

My friend refused to be comforted. "Audrey, if anything happened to you, I would just——"

"June." Mrs. Silverman appeared in the doorway, her several chins wobbling. "What did I tell you?"

June stared at her shoes. "We were just talking, Mommy."

But Mrs. Silverman took her daughter by the arm and dragged her away.

In the sanctuary, services had begun. Rabbi Grody was chanting, *"Shema Yisroel Adonai Eloheinu Adonai Echad."* "Hear O Israel, the Lord our God, the Lord is One" came back the weak response.

I took a seat between Tante and my father. He handed me a prayer book. The crooked Hebrew letters swam before me; tonight they looked ugly and strange. All of a sudden I wanted to be on the far side of that wall, watching a western with all those other folks.

The cavalry was thundering next door when the rabbi closed his prayer book, the sign that the sermon was about to begin. He looked at each of us, into every face, until the shul grew perfectly still, and the horses had faded away.

Then an amazing thing happened: Rabbi Grody began to cry. He put down his head and wept. When finally he wiped his eyes, he left the pulpit and came to stand in front of us. "Forgive me," he said, blowing his nose.

"What's to forgive?" a man called out.

The rabbi tucked his handkerchief into his robe. "No, I know, it's good to cry," he answered, as if this talking back and forth was something we always did. "It's necessary sometimes. That's not what I mean. I mean, forgive me for the swastika."

"It's not your fault, Rabbi." Mrs. Silverman's tone

said clearly whose fault she thought it was. My father sighed; Momma put a hand in his.

Rabbi Grody began to pace. "You know," he said, "it's the easiest thing in the world to blame someone else for what happens to you. That's what Adolf Hitler did, am I right?

"He said to the German people, 'You're poor? You're unhappy? It must be someone's fault. Who can we blame? I know, let's blame the Jews. It must be the Jews' fault.' And they believed him, didn't they?"

His upraised arms made wings of his wide sleeves. "I don't have to tell you what happened next. We've all read the newspapers and the history books. We've seen the pictures of bodies stacked in concentration camps. And we think that it is over, because it is only in books now, and we can forget the dead."

Tante leaned forward, gripping the pew. The rabbi addressed her in a voice hushed with respect. "I know this is painful, but it has to be said." He hesitated. "Pesel, I thought if you were among us, we would never forget. But I was wrong."

His eyes fell on me now, making me squirm. "A child came to see the swastika," he told the congregation. "She tried to help me. But I couldn't help her. I couldn't protect her. Do you know how that made me feel?"

A woman said, "Her father should have protected her in the first place."

"Her father," the rabbi corrected her, "is doing the best thing he can. He's trying to put an end to injustice. To prejudice. How many of us can say the same?"

"And what if we're scared?" Uncle Lewis asked from the back.

Rabbi Grody turned to me. "Were you scared, Audrey?"

I flushed. "Yes, sir."

"But you tried to help anyway?"

"I didn't think about it."

"There's your answer," he told my uncle.

His voice rose, full of feeling. "Now can you understand why I blame myself? Why didn't I stand up here, week after week, year after year, and remind us of the consequences of hatred? How could I forget the murder of six million of our people?"

A woman began to sob. Rabbi Grody brought his hands together. The sermon was over.

When my aunt rose to say Kaddish, we sat inside the immensity of her sorrow. And then it came to me why she prayed for the dead every Shabbos. She was a part of everything, just as Daddy had told me, part of all that had happened to her and the millions who had died.

Next thing I knew, I was on my feet reciting. Tante faltered and looked at me, a question in her eyes. Her confusion turned to wonder as Momma rose, and then Daddy, and a bunch of people behind him. Till everyone in shul was standing and chanting—even Mrs. Silverman—and we were all one voice, one prayer.

Afterward we filed into the muggy night. Blue halos circled the streetlights; the smell of rain was in the air. Main Street was deserted. The movie had not yet let out.

A few people came and clapped my father on the shoulder. Uncle Lewis held out a hand to him, his nose red from weeping, and the two brothers embraced. I looked for the Silvermans, but they had gone home.

Our calls of "Shabbat shalom" hung in the air. Daddy touched my shoulder. "Want to walk with me to get the car?" I nodded yes. "We'll be right back," he told Momma and Tante.

My aunt drew her shawl around her. "Wait. I come also." And the three of us set off down Main Street, me in the middle.

Tante's touch startled me. She'd slipped her hand into mine. I gazed up at her; her look back was shy. She squeezed my fingers and did not let go.

For a while all I knew was the unaccustomed feel of her hand around mine. I heard her say, "Nathan, I am ashamed of myself."

"Why, Tante?"

"You are so good to me, you and Selma both. You take me in when I have nothing. You treat me like a daughter. And how do I repay you? I am difficult. I say harsh things."

"Tante, I have a lot to learn," Daddy admitted. "I mean, you were right. You knew something like this would happen."

"All I am saying is, I will try to understand what you are doing. It is hard for me. Only do not ask me to be brave. This I cannot . . ."

I had stopped listening. At first they were just shadows in the shadows. Slowly my eyes made them out: two figures across the street keeping pace with us. "Daddy—"

"I see them, Audrey. Don't look, keep walking. Give me your hand."

Our Studebaker was half a block away when we saw that someone was sitting on the hood. An arm stuck out from the lamplit shade of an oak; it held a baseball bat.

Farther up, cones of light fell across Main Street. A car turned toward us, headlights in our eyes. It was Police Chief Monroe, doing his nightly rounds. The two figures fled; the one on the car slipped away too. The patrol car pulled alongside us. "Everything all right?" Mr. Monroe inquired.

"Two men were following us." My father squinted up the block. "They're gone now. And there was somebody on the car. With a bat."

Mr. Monroe frowned. "You get a look at him?"

Daddy shook his head. "He was partway in shadow."

"It was Buster LaCoste," I stated, calmer than I felt.

Three pairs of eyes turned on me. "Are you making this up?" the police chief demanded.

"I wouldn't do that—sir."

"Audrey, how do you know it was Buster?" Daddy asked.

"I recognized the scar on his arm."

"But did you see his face?"

"I know that scar, Daddy. It's just below his elbow on his right arm. And it's long and toothed."

Mr. Monroe worried his cheek. "Is that a fact?"

He stayed right where he was till we crossed to the car. In the streetlight, my aunt's face was blanched. We got in the back and Daddy drove to shul to pick up Momma and Joel. We were halfway home before I realized Tante's hand was still holding tightly onto mine.

My father went out soon after we got back. He didn't return for ages. I was still at my window when he hurried in, shoulders drooping. After a while the house grew silent again.

The sky was starless, raked with clouds. Pale thunderheads blew across the mountains toward the house. Sticks of lightning fell out of them; distant thunder growled. In the yard the wind raised the leaves, showing their silver undersides.

Fat drops of rain began to fall. A sheet of light brightened every blade of grass, followed by a crash close by. A shadow stole around the house, sending my heart into my mouth. A second flash revealed it to be Tante, making her blind way across the yard.

I hesitated a second. Then concern for my aunt overtook me and I leaped off the bed, hurrying down the stairs and into the kitchen. The back door was locked. My father must have bolted it when he came in; he'd never done that before.

I unlatched it and dashed out. Buckets of rain were falling, making it impossible to see. Suddenly lightning whitened the sky, silhouetting my aunt at the edge of the yard.

I crept toward her, pressing behind a tree when she turned, dropping to her knees. Her hands dug into the ground. She didn't seem to notice the rain soaking her to the skin. Lit by a blue bolt, her face was like marble, her eyes two moons in a frozen sky.

From my hiding place I saw her take the little doll from her sleeve and place it in the hole she'd dug. She buried it, covering it with dirt. Lightning flashed. As she raised her head, our eyes met for an instant before I ducked back behind the tree.

"Pesel?" she whispered, peering through a curtain of water. "Pesel? Is that you?"

The sound of rain pounded in my ears, drowning my thoughts. "Pesel," she called, more urgently.

I came around the tree. "No, Tante, it's me. It's Audrey."

Lightning gleamed, showing her puzzlement. "Pesel, why do you come?"

"Tante, please," I shouted over the roar of thunder. "I'm not Pesel, I'm Audrey."

Only my aunt was in a world of memory. She came toward me in the rain. "I thought to bury you," she cried. "To forget you. But no, you will not let me forget, will you?"

Dirt-caked fingers touched my head. "Your hair," she murmured. "Your beautiful hair."

"Tante, don't," I cried.

Lightning glimmered once, twice. She looked over her shoulder, as if we were being watched. "You should not be here, Pesel," she whispered. "They will see you. They will send you with us to the gas."

I shivered. "Tante, stop! Stop it!"

She clasped my shoulders. "Go, Pesel. Be like a

shadow. Don't let them catch you. Live, Pesel! Run!"

I ran. Somehow I found the cellar steps and stumbled down them. I raced through the basement and up the stairs, diving into my bed, my face in the pillow, while the storm crashed all around.

13

I didn't tell anyone about that night, not right away. For one thing, I couldn't think how I'd ever explain what had passed between me and my aunt.

But when Sam Cardwell dropped by a few days later to see how I was getting on, I found myself telling him everything. "And you know what bothers me most?" I asked as we walked out through fields of milkweed flowers and Queen Anne's lace.

Sam chewed a blade of grass. "What's that?"

"Just when it looked like Tante and me might start to be friends, Buster and those guys had to come ruin everything. They frightened her so bad, I think they set her off again."

He scratched his head. "I still don't get how come she thought you were her."

"I look a lot like she did when she was my age," I told him.

"But if you were her, who was she?"

"Good question. She was talking to herself, I guess. See, she gets confused in her mind sometimes, and then she can't tell what's the past and what's now. It's all the same to her."

We'd reached the pastures of the old Carrington farm.

A herd of cows watched us approach with soft mute eyes. "Come on," Sam said.

He talked to them slow and quiet while we wriggled under the barbed wire fence. Most sidestepped over the slope; the few that remained chewed their cud and paid us no mind.

We took off our shoes, splashing in the zigzagging creek, then settled in the shade of a lone elm. Above us an oriole piped its cheerful summer song. Sam stretched out on his stomach.

I picked up the conversation. "And you know what else? I think I know now why me and Tante never got along. I probably remind her too much of who she used to be. It must hurt just to look at me."

"I can understand that," he teased.

"Shut up," I answered, laughing, and lay back in the grass. Over the rise a little fleet of clouds puffed gently along. Dragonflies whirred like tiny helicopters above the cropped grass. Soft fingers of breeze tickled my cheek.

"Sam?" I asked in a dreamy voice. "You ever wonder how come you were born a Negro? You know what I mean? Like the way I was born Jewish?"

He grinned. "Just lucky, I guess."

"I'm serious. How come some people are victims, and some aren't?"

"Who you calling a victim, girl?"

"Well, what would you call getting beat up?"

Sam rolled over on his back. "You may not believe it, Audrey, but this is the best time of my life."

I looked at him. "You're right, I don't believe it."

He sat up, arms around his knees. "My whole life, this

is what we been talking about. How we going to make things better? When's it going to start? And now it's here, it's started."

"Sam, you don't really think Mr. Monroe's going to hire your daddy."

"It doesn't matter."

"You don't mean that."

"Yes, I do. All that matters is that we're trying. So long as we keep on, sooner or later something's got to give. Those people in Montgomery never thought the boycott would go on for so long, but it has."

"It's kind of like a miracle, huh?"

"Except it's not a miracle," Sam exclaimed, "it's just work! See, them folks down there, they got a preacher, name of Martin Luther King, Jr. And he's been telling them they can have their rights, without raising their fists or hurting anybody. It's a thing called nonviolence."

"But what if someone hurts you first?"

"Fighting back isn't going to help us, Audrey. There's all kinds of ways to fight. You got to use your mind, not your fists." He tapped his feet in excitement. "Get this. Every Wednesday night at church Reverend Hutcherson schools us in nonviolence."

"Really? How do you mean?"

"He shows us what to do if someone calls you a name. Or tries to get in your face. How to act peaceful and not let them get you riled."

"Like what? Show me."

Sam got up. "I'm still getting the hang of it but—" He cocked his head. "You hear something?"

I listened: A sound like drums beating rose behind the

hill. The ground began to shake. The oriole flew off, shrieking, as twenty cows stampeded down the rise toward us, nostrils flared, eyes wild.

Sam pulled me to my feet. "Get up the tree! Quick!"

I flung my arms around a branch, swung myself over it, and held on for dear life. Sam clambered up after me.

The herd ran under us, hooves pounding where we'd sat not seconds before. On the far side of the creek they slowed, stamping and snorting in a cloud of dust.

"Goodness!" I cried. "What brought that on?"

Above me Sam jerked his head. "Look yonder."

Buster LaCoste ambled over the slope, waving a stick and singing as he came. "Jew and a nigger sitting in a tree, k-i-s-s-i-n-g."

"You could've killed us!" I shouted.

"Aww." One of Buster's eyes was blackened; there were bruises all along his cheek. He circled the elm, thwacking at our feet with the stick. "Guess you're up a tree now, aren't you, Red?"

"Quit!" I yanked my feet out of reach.

Sam called down, "Audrey! Climb up here! Come on!"

I started up, legs trembling. Buster beat on the trunk. "Careful," he said sarcastically. "Wouldn't do to have you fall and bust your head."

"Go away, you idiot."

"Audrey, just get up here," Sam commanded. And pretty soon I was sitting beside him in the crown of the tree.

Buster yelled, "Why'd you have to rat on me, Red? I know it was you."

"Mr. Monroe told?"

"Didn't have to," he replied. "I saw you talking to him. You and your daddy and that crazy crow. Came to my house the next day, asking questions. My daddy beat me for it too. Not for what I did," he added. "For getting caught."

"Should have locked you up," I told him.

"Isn't against the law to sit on a car. What's the matter, Leroy?" he sneered at Sam. "Cat got your tongue?"

Sam fixed his eyes on the hills and said nothing.

"Hey, nigger," Buster taunted. "Why don't you come down and let me knock your block off? Look here!" He threw away the stick. "I fight fair."

Still Sam stared straight ahead and did not respond.

"What's the problem?" Buster yelled at him. "You chicken? You yellow? Hey, you can't be yellow, you're black!" And he hooted like that was the funniest thing a body ever said.

I couldn't contain myself. "Shut up, you worthless piece of protoplasm."

Sam nudged me with his foot. "Audrey, be still."

Buster mocked me. "'Shut up, you worthless.' Red, how come you always act like you're better than me? You think I'm dumb as dirt, don't you?"

I opened my mouth to agree. Sam shook his head.

"Well, I'm not!" Buster's voice rose in fury. "Come on down, nigger, like I said. I'll show you who's dumb!" He whirled and picked up a rock. "Here, I'll make you come down!"

"Oh, don't," I choked.

Buster threw the rock. It thunked on a branch above us and bounced to the ground.

"Quit," I yelled.

"Think I'm stupid? Think I'm garbage?" Buster shouted as another rock whistled past my ear.

"Audrey, do like this." Sam curled up like a sow bug, wrapping his arms around his head.

"Think I'm nothing but dog doo, don't you?" Buster kept on.

Thud! A rock cracked against the branch I was sitting on. I scrunched up like Sam said.

"I know you do!" Buster screamed. "Everybody does!" *Thud!* came a rock against Sam's hand. He winced and covered it with the other.

Buster was working himself into a lather. "My daddy thinks so too! I can't do anything right!" *Thud!* A rock hit my sneaker; I bit my lip to keep from crying out.

"Beats me and locks me in a closet!" Buster shrieked. "Says I deserve it!" *Thud!* "Because I'm stupid!" *Thud!* "I'm garbage!" *Thud!* "I'm—"

Suddenly it was quiet, save for the drone of dragonflies, my own ragged breathing, and a strange hiccuping sound. I peeked between my arms.

Buster had wore himself out. His face was streaked with sweat and tears. "I'm dirt," he muttered, throwing a rock at his feet. Then without a glance at Sam or me, he turned and walked away.

Sam followed him with his eyes till he was just a speck on the horizon. "You okay?" he asked me.

"Tolerable." I was shaking so bad, I could hardly talk.

Sam helped me down. His shirt was ripped, his hand puffy and bleeding.

I wiped my nose on my arm. "You must think I'm a big baby."

"Not me," he answered. "I know exactly how you feel."

We looked at each other. Then I started for home. I was under the barbed wire when Sam yelled, "You did good, Audrey Ina!" and disappeared over the rise.

The house was still when I slipped inside. I could hear Frances down in the laundry room, singing to herself. Momma and Joel were napping; Daddy and Tante were at work. I eased myself into a tub of hot water and sat there a long time, glad for the peace and quiet.

Afterward I went out back. The sky was white with heat. Faint thunder rumbled, reminding me once more of the night my aunt had mistaken me for Pesel. I stood over the bare earth where the little doll was buried. Nothing could grow there now, I thought, and started to cry.

Before I knew it, I'd dropped to my knees and was digging into the dirt. Soon I was holding the little doll in my hand. Soil clung to its face and hair, but the eyes stared back unchanged.

The strangest sensation came over me then. It was almost as if I knew how it felt to be Pesel in Auschwitz— head shaved, carving this little figure out of her loneliness and loss. And suddenly I understood why she'd made the doll. She must have known the girl she'd been was lost forever, would never return. She'd made it as a reminder of who she once was, so she'd never forget her.

Time fell away. I didn't hear my daddy and my aunt come home. I wasn't aware of anything except the doll in my hand.

Tante's shriek jarred me back to the yard. I turned to find her racing toward me on a wave of fury.

14

You take a soft-boiled egg traveling at the speed of light. Now according to Dr. Einstein's special theory of relativity, time—to us on Earth anyway—would appear to slow down for that egg.

Say you start soft boiling two eggs at the same moment, one here on Earth, and the other out in space moving at the speed of light. Since three minutes at the speed of light would seem to take longer, compared to three Earth minutes, by the time that outer space egg is done, the egg on Earth would be hard-boiled. Dr. Einstein called that a paradox.

A paradox is when two different things happen at once and both appear true. That's how it was, watching Tante approach me. Her journey took seconds, but it felt like forever.

One thing was certain: My egg was cooked. My aunt stood over me, terrible to behold. She dug her fingers into my shoulders. "How dare you!"

"I'm sorry," I cried. "Tante, please, you're hurting me."

She shook me so hard my teeth rattled. "Thief! You have no right!"

"Tante, stop. Stop it!"

She froze, anger melting into amazement. Her hands

flew to her mouth. "It was you," she whispered. "In the rain. It was you."

"Yes," I gasped.

She took me by the arms. "Why were you there?"

"I saw you from my window," I confessed. "I followed you."

"It was you," she echoed, stumbling back, sinking into the grass. "I thought you were a ghost."

I sat beside her. After a minute she took the doll from my hand. "Poor Pesel," she murmured, brushing dirt from its face. "Hitler destroyed you once. Now I try also."

"Maybe she's stronger than you think," I ventured.

Her eyes flickered over me. "Did I frighten you?"

"Which time?"

A laugh burst out of her, short and rueful. "You do not mind this fear. You have such courage. Not like me. I am a coward."

"You?" I looked her full in the face. "Tante, I think you're the bravest person I've ever known."

"You do not know what you are talking about."

"But—" I hesitated. "How else could you have survived Auschwitz?"

"Many brave people died at Auschwitz," she answered. "It has nothing to do with courage."

She looked away. "When I know my family is going to die," she whispered, "I want to die also."

Her words began to pour out, as through a hole in time. "The Nazis put me in the line to work. Because I am tall for my age, and strong. And a woman in a striped uniform tells me, 'You are one of the lucky ones.' She points to the line where Mama and Tata and Gitel are standing. 'Those people there,' she says, 'they are going to die.' "

She shuddered. "When I hear this, I do not care what happens to me. I leave my line and run to Mama. I am so afraid. I know I cannot live without them."

She lifted her hands, the way she'd done to me that night in the rain. "Mama takes me by the shoulders. 'No, Pesel,' she tells me. 'If I must die, it will be easier knowing a part of me still lives. Live, Pesel. As long as you are alive, we are also.'

"And she sends me back alone. To live. I never see her again." Her face fell into her hands. "I am so ashamed."

"Why?"

"I wanted to die. Only because of Mama am I alive. Only for her am I here."

"Then I'm grateful to her." A tear rolled down my cheek.

She peered at me, baffled. "Why do you cry?"

"Because I'm sad for you."

"No." She shook her head. "Cry for Mama. Cry for Gitel. I do not deserve such feelings."

"I'm crying for them too."

She didn't answer, but sat and gazed into the distance. Finally, she said, "You are a funny girl, Audrey Ina." Her voice had a tender ring I'd never heard before.

"Do you forgive me?" I asked.

"For what?"

"What I mean is—do you think you and I—could be friends?"

"Friends?" she repeated, as if the word were new to her. "Why not?"

June twilights last forever. Wisps of coral and rose hung over the mountains when my father found me in the yard that night, close to eight o'clock. I'd been under the sweet gum since supper, watching the opal sky darken and Tante's lamplight come on.

We lay in the grass surrounded by a hundred fiddling crickets. A whippoorwill called once, twice, from the field. Above us reigned a quartermoon; Arcturus shone like a topaz to the north.

"Daddy? Can I ask you a personal question?"

He opened his arms. "Fire away."

"Do you believe in God?"

"What makes you ask?"

"Well, I've been sitting here thinking about Tante. And I've been thinking about God too. And I can't understand how He could have let a place like Auschwitz happen."

My father nodded. "I wondered when we'd have this conversation." He sat up. "I don't understand it either."

"But you believe in Him anyway?"

"I do." He gazed up. "You know, maybe it isn't God who's responsible for these things, Audrey. Maybe we are. And what He did was grant us the ability to choose. We can do evil—or we can choose not to."

"But Tante didn't get to choose anything. She was just a kid."

He rubbed his face. "I don't have all the answers, honey. I don't know why there has to be so much pain in the world."

The moon set, spangling the sky with stars. A meteor spilled from the cup of the Big Dipper, leaving no traces.

I kept my eyes heavenward. "But then, Daddy? How do you know for certain there is a God?"

"I don't," he replied. "I have to go on faith. On the still small voice inside me that says it must be so."

He went on. "That shooting star makes me think of something a Jewish writer named Martin Buber wrote. Someone asked him how he knew what the Word of God was. These aren't his exact words, but he said it was kind of like a meteor. You can see its path across the sky, but you won't ever find the stone that made it. Can you understand that?"

"Did he mean God is a mystery, but there are signs?"

My daddy smiled. "What makes you so smart?"

I smiled back and we sat in easy silence till Tante's light flicked off. "Daddy?" I whispered. "Do you think Tante believes in God?"

"I don't know."

"She told me once she didn't believe in anything."

"That doesn't surprise me."

"But still she goes to shul and prays." I sighed. "It's all so confusing."

Daddy said, "I guess it's like Einstein's theory of relativity, Audrey. How things look to you depends on where you're standing. Everyone has their own way of seeing the world, depending on the life they were born into, and the things that happen to them. If you really want to know someone like Tante, you have to put yourself in her shoes. You have to try and see things from where she stands."

"It's funny you should say that, Daddy. Because lately I've been feeling like maybe the war happened to me too. Not in the same way as Tante, of course. But there are times I feel so badly for her, it feels like her pain is mine. Does that sound crazy?"

He took my hand. "Not at all. What you're talking about is compassion. Knowing that what happens to one person happens to us all."

I thought about that. "But, Daddy? How do you feel compassion toward someone who wants to hurt you?"

His brow dipped. "Are you talking about someone in particular?"

Much as I'd dreaded telling him about Buster, I knew I had to. When I'd finished, he said, "Audrey, don't expect me not to tell Elmo about this."

"Well, don't expect me to have compassion for that Buster."

"Sounds to me, honey, like Buster's a victim too," my daddy answered. "Look, I don't like the things he does, but try standing in his shoes a minute. Think what it must be like for him, being treated so cruelly by his own father. His daddy hits him, so he strikes out at you and Sam."

I shook my head. "He acts so cocky, I never knew he felt so bad about himself. I used to make fun of him all the time for being slow," I admitted.

"Well, maybe now you'll be more tolerant."

"Okay, but, Daddy, he's still dangerous. I mean, did you feel compassion for the Nazis?"

"No," he answered. "I guess it's hard to feel anything but animosity toward your enemies. But maybe we shouldn't think of Buster as an enemy. Maybe we should think of him as someone who's in pain."

He raked his hair. "I'll tell you what I do hate, Audrey. I hate putting you in this danger."

"You're in danger too."

He leaned back in the grass. After a time he said, "During the war there were a few heroic people who came to the aid of the Jews. But for the most part, the world sat back and did nothing. Even among the Jews in this country—and I'm ashamed to include myself—there was no outcry to speak of.

"So when I see people like the Cardwells trying to change the injustices against them, I can't keep quiet anymore. I couldn't live with myself if I did. Because I think it could happen again. Maybe not to us, but to someone—"

I finished his thought. "And if it happens to them, it happens to us too."

He pulled me into his arms. "Listen to me, Audrey. Blue Gap is still our home. And there are a lot of people here who care about us, who want us to be safe. Do you believe me?"

I leaned back against him. "I want to."

"Look!" His arm shot up toward a meteor streaking across a flap of night, followed by two more arrows of fire.

"It's a sign, Daddy," I cried.

"It's a mystery," he agreed.

15

I was on my way downtown to meet Tante after work. Far as we knew, the parade was still a go, and with the Fourth of July only three days away, she'd agreed to help me with my costume.

Frances boarded the bus too, to keep an eye on me till I got off at Marylou's. Momma had arranged for Uncle Lewis to pick my aunt and me up at five thirty sharp and carry us home.

I started to the back with Frances. She shook her head. "Uh-uh, no ma'am. You sit down front."

"But Frances—"

"Audrey Ina, let's not draw any more attention to ourselves than we have to."

I took a seat in the middle and gazed out the window. Blue Gap was decked out for the holiday. Patriotic banners hung from houses; streetlights and traffic lights were draped with festive streamers. On Church Street the red-and-white-striped barber pole was festooned with blue paper stars.

I glanced back. All the seats in the Negro section were filled, so Frances had to stand, even though there were plenty of empty seats by me.

The bus lurched to the curb and Edwina Clark got on. I hadn't seen that girl since the day of the swastika.

I knew my daddy would want me to have compassion

for Edwina, but we had a score to settle first. I stole over behind her. Leaning forward, I whispered, "You ain't going to heaven."

She jumped. "Oh! You scared the daylights out of me!"

"Liars can't get in," I kept on.

"I don't know what you're talking about, Audrey Stern," she said back.

"You do so, Edwina Clark. You know Buster threw dirt in the rabbi's whitewash on purpose. I didn't make him do it."

"Didn't say you did," she threw over her shoulder.

"That's right, you didn't say a word. And that's as bad as a lie when you know something's true. That was sinful of you, Edwina. Guess I'll be seeing you in you-know-where."

She spun around. "Oh, you make me sick! You and that rude mother of yours! Talking about Jesus like she knew him! I bet she dyes her hair!"

"Does not!"

"Does too! Jews can't have blond hair."

"Says who?"

"My cousin Yvonne. She's a beautician. She says all Jew hair is black."

I held up my red locks. "What do you call this?"

"Well." Edwina bit her lip. "Maybe you're adopted."

I busted out laughing.

"What is so funny?" she spat. "Oh, I hate you, I just hate you! Sometimes I wish Mr. Monroe *would* cancel the parade, just to spite you!"

I looked at Edwina's small, pinched face; half the time she didn't even know what she was talking about. "Well,

I hope it's not canceled," I told her, more quietly now. "Because lots of folks would be disappointed, including you."

"Like who?" she sneered. "Your friend, little black Sambo?"

I bristled. "For your information, his name is Sam. And now that you mention it, yeah, he'd be sorry too."

"Boo-hoo on that nigger."

The bus swung onto Main Street; my stop was next. I stood and pulled on the cord. Then I bent down. "In case you hadn't noticed, Edwina," I whispered in her ear, "you got the same feelings as a Negro."

Sending Frances a wave, I sashayed down the aisle. On the curb I waved again as the bus pulled away. There went Edwina, staring straight ahead, looking like she'd just sucked a lemon.

The bells on the door of Marylou's tinkled my arrival. "Well, look who's here," Miss Farley said, sliding four crisp dollar bills across the counter toward my aunt.

"Hey, Miss Farley. Hey, Tante." I gave my aunt a private smile of hello.

She looked relieved to see me. "How was the bus?"

"Piece of cake," I replied. "Matter of fact, I had an edifying conversation with an old acquaintance of mine."

The librarian smiled. "I understand I'm not the only one being outfitted for the parade."

"Who you going as this year, Miss Farley?" In summers past she'd gone as Calamity Jane and Madame Curie. Three years ago her Marie Antoinette had a towering wig that swirled like soft ice cream.

Now she held up a shimmering white dress trimmed in gold. "Who do you think?"

"Ooh, must be an angel."

Miss Farley humphed. "No one would recognize me, that's for sure." She put the dress against her and lifted a hand over her head. "Now can you guess?"

"Jeepers, I'm stumped."

Tante recited: "Give me your tired, your poor, your huddled masses yearning to breathe free—"

"Oh, I know!" I exclaimed. "The Statue of Liberty."

Miss Farley nodded. "And see what your clever aunt did?" She showed me a cardboard crown spray painted light green and a torch with orange cellophane for a flame.

"I can't wait to see it all on," I told her.

"Don't tell a soul," she breathed. "I simply want to dazzle them." She peered over her glasses. "I have a few other surprises up my sleeve too."

"We're all ears," I said.

"I'll give you a hint," she answered. "*You* inspired me."

"Me?"

"Yes, you, Audrey Stern. And your father and Lovelle Cardwell, of course. I wish you could have heard your daddy speak before town council the other night. My, he was eloquent."

My folks had thought it best if I did not attend that meeting, but Daddy told me about it afterward. Reverend Hutcherson and the rabbi had presented a petition in favor of Mr. Cardwell, signed by everybody in both congregations, and others in the community too, including Miss Farley.

Then council did vote. And though it came out 3 to 2 against supporting Mr. Cardwell, my father was encouraged that at least one other councilman besides himself had come over to Mr. Cardwell's side.

The librarian said now, "That night I told myself, Henrietta Farley, if they've got the gumption, so do you."

She picked up her packages. "Thanks again, Miss Minkowitz. Tootle-loo, Audrey. By the way, who you going as?"

I grinned at Tante. "I have my surprises too."

Miss Farley chortled. "Well, come see me. Don't forget. I want to view you in all your glory. I'll be out in front of the library all afternoon." The bells rang lightly and she was gone.

Tante put out the CLOSED sign and locked the front door. In all the years we'd known each other, my aunt and I had never spent much time together. Now I felt grown-up being there alone with her.

I followed her through the beaded curtain into the backroom where the sewing machines sat. Mannequins stood sentry over a scattered landscape of fabrics and spools of thread. Laces and feathers were pinned to the walls, and the ceiling was a billowing sky of netting and scarves.

Tante held out a roll of thick silvery cotton. "So what do you think of this?"

"Ooh," I replied, passing a hand over it. "It's perfection."

"It does not breathe, this fabric, so it will be hot for you."

"So long as you can make it look like a spacesuit, I don't care."

She fanned a hand. "Piece of pie."

"Cake," I corrected her. "I just want it to look cosmic. And wait till you see the helmet I'm making to go with it."

"Come," she said. "I must take your measurements."

She stood me on a stool and I watched as she snapped the tape and scribbled figures on a scrap of fabric. "Do you like to sew?" I asked her.

She shrugged, kneeling to measure my ankle. "It is what I do."

"Did your mother teach you?" It popped out uninvited.

Her face darkened. "You ask too many questions."

"I'm sorry, I—"

She held up a hand to shush me. After a while she said in a low voice, "Mama was a magician. I believe this. Gitel and I are sure she sews in her sleep, because everything she makes is a dream."

She paused. "Especially I remember the gowns. For dancing."

"You went dancing?"

"Not me," she answered. "That is, yes, we dance. But we are poor Jews, we dance in our aprons. The gowns are for the rich."

Her eyes glowed. "Oh, the brocades, the satins Mama used! All stitched by hand, every stitch perfect. Sometimes she would sew pearls into the bodice. Real pearls from the Atlantic Ocean! Can you imagine this?"

"Who were they for?"

She dropped her voice. "The baroness."

"The baroness?"

"Near Jarzyna is an ancient castle," she explained. "And in it lives an ancient Polish nobleman." She smiled. "Sometimes Gitel and I would go with Mama in the wagon. When she brought the gowns to his wife."

I could almost hear the clackety-clack of horse's hooves on stones. And I could picture the two sisters bouncing in the wagon, Pesel's hair flashing like a new penny in the sun.

"This one morning we go and the baroness is at breakfast. In a big room with many—how do you say?— chandeliers. All alone at a long table. With two men playing the violin."

"While she's having breakfast? Ooh, how romantic."

"She is *meshugge*," Tante replied, making us both laugh. "I should not say this," she went on. "She is very fond of Mama. And us girls. She wants to take Gitel—"

"How do you mean, take her?"

Tante sighed. "To hide her from Hitler. Some Polish people do this to help the Jews. If a child looks Aryan— like Gitel does—they take her and say that she is theirs. So the Nazis will not persecute her."

I sat on the stool. "Why didn't she do it?"

"Tata could not let Gitel go. He thinks we will be all right and better for us to be together." She shuddered. "I cannot think what Tata's heart is saying to him when he stands beside Gitel in the gas."

I covered my eyes at the image. "Enough," my aunt declared, rising. "Audrey, I am so selfish. I do not think how this talk will hurt you."

I tried to sit her back down. "It's all right. Really."

She pulled away. "No. It is not all right."

"Tante, listen. Maybe Pesel's dead to you, but not to me. I feel like I know her."

"You cannot know her."

"I want to."

She turned away. For a long time she said nothing. Then slowly, her hand moving absently over scraps of lace, she began to describe the barracks where she had lived with other female prisoners in Auschwitz.

"At night we sleep side by side on bare wooden planks. No pillow, no blanket. In the morning, always, someone is dead. Sometimes it is the person next to you."

She saw me cringe. "Yes. They die from cold or sickness or hunger. Or because their heart is so broken."

My mind traveled to the bleak buildings where the bodies were piled outside the door each morning. "And those are the good nights," my aunt droned.

Other nights the Nazis made them stand outside for hours, shivering in the winter wind. All around her, prisoners dropped from exhaustion. Those who fell were sent to the gas chamber.

"But not me," Tante said. "I tell myself I do not feel the cold, I am not tired."

"Why did they make you do that?"

"Sometimes there is a reason. Maybe because one of us tries to escape. Other times, no reason. Perhaps they are curious to see how much we want to live."

Morning brought breakfast. "A slice of bread, thin like paper." Her voice made me feel the tasteless mix of flour and sawdust against my own tongue. I saw Pesel breaking hers into smaller and smaller pieces, to make it seem like more than it was. Lunch and dinner were a watery soup with a few rotten vegetables thrown in.

From morning to night she worked, sewing for an *oberscharführerin*, a female Nazi officer. "She has me make clothes for her children in Germany," Tante recalled. "Where do they think these clothes come from? Do they wear them to parties, these dresses made in hell?"

She frowned. "This woman is very beautiful. And very cruel. Every day she sends people to the gas. But I am useful to her, so she keeps me. All I do is sew. With every stitch I hear Mama's voice, telling me to live. Some days I cannot remember if I am dead or alive. I say to myself, if I am sewing I must be alive."

She drifted into silence. "And the doll?" I asked, after a moment. "How were you able to make her?"

"I steal a scrap of wood from my work," she explained. "And the thread also. This is very dangerous thing to do. I can be killed for this. I do it because I have to. I must have one thing that is mine."

She gazed down at her hands. "I do not think when I am making her, that I am making Pesel. But that is what comes. When I look at her, I can pretend for one moment how it feels to have hair. To have my family alive and near me . . ."

Her eyes brimmed with tears. She brushed them away with the back of her hand. "Come. We clean up. Lewis will be here soon."

I rose reluctantly and took the broom she handed me. She began to neaten rolls of fabric. I glanced at her. "Tante? Can I ask you a personal question?"

She threw me a look. "Audrey, all you know how to ask is personal questions."

"Do you mind?"

"I am trying to get used to it."

"The thing is, I was just wondering, it doesn't hurt you to sew now?"

"At first, yes," she answered. "When I am out of the camp, I think I cannot sew. That it will remind me too much of Auschwitz. But I find it does not matter. *Everything* reminds me of Auschwitz."

16

Tante's watch said five thirty when she locked the back door of Marylou's behind us. We dropped a sack of scraps into a garbage can and started down the alley toward Main.

Two men slouched around the corner, blocking our path. "Going someplace?" the first one asked. His hat was pulled over his face, but I knew the voice immediately; he was the man on the phone. With him was a tall, loose-jointed fellow.

Tante pulled me to her, her grip like iron as a third grizzled man crept up behind us, trapping us between. "What do you want?" she demanded.

"We just want to visit with you," the man in the hat said. "We thought maybe you could talk some sense into that Jew Stern."

"I know you," I blurted out. "You're the one who called us."

"Audrey, *sha*," my aunt hissed.

He smiled like a shark. "I see you've got company," he remarked to Tante. "What the heck, the more the merrier. Of course we weren't expecting his bigmouthed daughter."

He moved in closer and the others followed, making a

tight circle around us. "Kind of changes things, doesn't it, boys?" he sneered. "Gives me an idea. Like what would hurt her daddy most?" And with that he grabbed me by the hair and pulled me to him.

"Ow!" I shouted, struggling. "Turn me loose!"

Tante reached into her bag and drew out a pair of long sharp scissors. She slashed them through the air, making the other two men jump back.

"Grab her, you idjits!" the hat man hollered.

"Not a good idea," a deep, familiar voice said. It was Mr. Cardwell, coming down the alley toward us.

His sudden appearance startled my aunt. She turned the scissors on him instead. "Tante, no!" I cried.

"You can put them scissors away, Miss Minkowitz." Mr. Cardwell kept his voice even. "What you got to pick on a little girl for?" he asked the hat man. "You want to hurt someone, hurt me."

"Look out!" I shouted as the grizzled man lunged. But Sam's daddy sidestepped him with surprising agility for so large a person.

Now the tall one charged him. Only Mr. Cardwell flipped him over his arm like he was a rag doll, and left him lying in a blinking daze. When he saw that, the grizzled man took off down the alley.

Feeling his grip loosen, I gave the hat man a backward kick in the shin. He yelped off, bumping smack into Mr. Monroe who'd run in from the street.

The police chief got him by the collar. "What's going on here?" he demanded.

Tante hastily slipped the scissors back in her bag.

"That woman's crazy," the hat man whined to Mr. Monroe. "She pulled a sharp object on us."

"Don't suppose you gave her reason." The police chief gave his collar a yank.

"Hey!" he responded. "We were just having a friendly conversation—"

"Friendly?" I snorted. Tante clapped a hand on my shoulder.

The police chief eyed me. "How come you always manage to be where there's trouble?"

"Mr. Monroe, I swear, we were just minding our own business! And if Mr. Cardwell hadn't come along, there's no telling what might have happened."

"I'll tell you what happened." The hat man pointed to Mr. Cardwell. "That nigger attacked poor Slim."

Mr. Cardwell knocked the dust from his hat. "Mr. Stern asked would I check on them on my way home," he explained to Mr. Monroe. "And when I come down the alley, there were three men here. That one had Audrey by the hair, and the other two had Miss Minkowitz cornered."

"Kind of hard to corner someone with scissors in her hand," the police chief commented.

My aunt reddened. "I am a seamstress. I keep scissors in my bag."

From between two garbage cans, Slim tried to pull himself up. "Where you going?" Mr. Monroe growled at him. "I ain't finished with you yet."

He turned to Mr. Cardwell. "Think you can help me get him to the car?"

"Yes, sir," he replied.

Tante took me by the hand. "Come, Audrey, we go home." She hesitated. "Mr. Monroe?"

"Yes, Miss Minkowitch?"

She drew herself up. "These men come to do us harm. Then I am glad I am a seamstress."

That night I had a dream.

A spaceship from the Big Dipper lands behind our house, bright as a Ferris wheel and twice as big. Aliens with kind faces roam its corridors, waiting for me to board.

Everyone has come to see me off: the Cardwells, June, Rabbi Grody, Miss Farley, even the police chief has showed. Dr. Einstein is there too, white-haired and smiling.

I greet him. "Dr. Einstein? Can I ask you a personal question?"

He regards me. "Is there any other kind?"

"Have you ever traveled at the speed of light?"

"Many times," he answers without hesitation.

"Ooh, what's it like?"

"$E = mc^2$."

I blink. "Come again?"

His smile is sweet. "Remember, the speed of light is the one unchanging thing in the entire universe. Why this should be so is a great mystery. And I believe that if anything else travels at this remarkable speed, its mass will grow until it becomes infinite."

"But isn't that impossible?"

He holds up a finger. "Exactly."

"Then how can you travel that fast?"

He taps his forehead. "With my mind. The mind can go anywhere, Audrey, at any speed. Maybe faster than the speed of light."

"So are you saying the mind is infinite?"

"What makes you so smart?"

"If that's true," I reflect, "then the mind must contain everything in the universe."

He chuckles. "You have to admit it's an interesting theory."

"Does it apply to soft-boiled eggs too?"

"Absolutely." And off he goes for a look at Brother's bugs.

It's hard for me to say good-bye, but secretly I am thrilled to be going. "Where's Tante?" I keep asking, only nobody seems to know.

At last the captain comes to the door of the spaceship. "It's time, Audrey Ina," she announces.

I give Momma one last hug and start up the ramp, feeling my feet leave the Earth. Humming deliciously, the ship lifts off the ground.

All at once Tante tears out of the house, wooden box in hand. "Audrey, wait! I come with you!"

I fall back to Earth with a crash. Somebody screams. Footsteps pound down a hill. "Fire!" my father shouts.

I bolted up in bed, wide awake. "Fire!" Daddy yelled again from downstairs.

Now I could hear the rush of flames. The hallway was lit by a leaping orange glow. Like two converging winds,

Momma whirled down the stairs as my aunt came up from the basement. Together they ran into the living room.

Joel appeared at my door, his face white. I picked him up. "I'm here, Brother."

His arms around my neck, we inched down the stairs. Flames engulfed the curtains, making a roaring border around where the bay window used to be.

"Don't come in!" Momma screamed. "There's glass everywhere!"

Their bare feet cut and bleeding, my parents were beating at the fire with pillows off the sofa, a throw rug from the floor. Tante had taken a blanket from her room; she at least was wearing shoes.

The sofa burst into flames, making a curious curling sound. "I'll call the fire department," I yelled. Joel on my hip, I staggered to the phone. "They're coming," I reported back breathlessly.

The carpet had started to burn, hungry fingers of flame licking this way and that. "Audrey, go outside with Joel," Daddy panted, "and turn on the garden hose—"

"Nathan." My mother turned; the hem of her nightgown had caught fire. Flames billowed up her body and into her hair with a horrifying *whoosh*.

"Momma!" Joel shrieked.

With one bound Tante folded Momma into the blanket and rolled her onto the floor, extinguishing the flames. Then my father picked her up, blanket and all, and carried her from the house.

"Go!" my aunt thundered, pushing me and Joel out.

Daddy lay Momma in the grass, where she moaned

inside the smoking blanket. Tante brushed singed hair off my mother's forehead, murmuring to her in Polish. Joel buried his head in my side and could not stop crying.

A fire engine came wailing down Westerly Drive, an ambulance close behind. In no time at all, hoses were hooked to the hydrant and water was cascading into the house.

The doctor wrapped Daddy's cut feet. Two men put Momma onto a stretcher and lifted her into the van. Her eyes sought Tante's. "Look after them," she mouthed.

Tears slid down my aunt's cheeks. "I will, Selma."

My father took Joel in his arms. "I'm going with Momma to the hospital," he told us.

I threw myself at him. "Let me come with you."

"No, you stay here with Tante and Brother." He turned to my aunt. "I'll call you."

"All right, Nathan." She gathered Joel and me to her.

Then my father limped into the ambulance and we watched as the siren and pulsing lights faded up the road.

Clouds of smoke rose from the living room long after the firemen had gone. The ceiling dripped; drops of water clung to shattered glass and shone in the light of the moon.

Mr. Monroe came by, kicking through the wet ash till he found pieces of a broken pop bottle. Someone had filled it with gasoline and put in a rag, setting the cloth on fire before throwing the whole thing through the window.

Uncle Lewis showed up then, wanting us to spend the night at his house. Only Joel refused to leave. He was sure Momma was coming back and no one had the heart to tell him otherwise.

The police chief parked his car across the street, settling in till dawn. None of us wanted to go back in the house yet, so we four sat numbly in the yard a time. The trees were phantoms against the sky, the Big Dipper a question mark in the endless night.

17

"Why can't I go to the hospital with you?" I asked Daddy for the umpteenth time the following Sunday morning.

"Because." He flipped his tie to knot it. "I already told you. They don't allow visitors under twelve."

"We could fib. I'm tall for my age."

"Wrong." My father looked harried. I'd hardly seen him since the night of the fire. For two days now, he'd straggled in late from the hospital and was gone first thing the next morning.

Momma was in serious condition. She had third-degree burns on her face and arms, and there was a deep, dangerous burn on her leg. The doctor said she'd pull through, but she'd have to be in the hospital for some time more.

I trailed my father down the stairs. The living room was cleaned up now. Mr. Cardwell and Sam had carted away the rubble. Before they left, they'd draped a white sheet over the empty window; it gave the house a blind, lonely look.

In the kitchen Tante greeted Daddy and me, Frances's flowered apron tied around her waist. She was rearranging pans on a counter already crowded with casseroles and pie plates.

"Let me guess." My father lifted foil off a still-warm apple crisp. "More food came."

Since that first morning food had arrived in an unending stream. "Look in the fridge." My aunt sounded awed. "I think maybe we open a restaurant."

The refrigerator was packed with dishes, each with a note attached. "We're praying for you," said one, on a half-eaten pot of stewed yams. It was from Reverend Hutcherson and his family.

Miss Farley had brought over six jars of her boysenberry jam. Neighbors and friends we didn't even know we had, had sent the rest. My father was right about one thing: A lot of people did care about us.

Tante handed him a cup of coffee. "How was Selma last night?"

"Restless but all right." He gulped the coffee down. "I best get going."

"What about breakfast?"

"I'll grab something at the hospital."

"Nathan, please, there is so much here. You should eat, you look terrible." He did not answer. She sighed. "All right, I know. Give Selma my love."

"Tante, come quick!" Joel shouted through the screen door. In Momma's absence, Brother was sticking to my aunt like glue. "My callerpittars!"

She ran out, Daddy and me behind. Joel's bugs had grown as plump as my pinky finger. My aunt had fashioned a cage for them out of an old hatbox of Momma's, stretching wedding veil netting over the cutout sides.

Now some of the caterpillars hung upside down from the ceiling of the cage, curled on themselves like seashells. Others were already enclosed in tiny jade-green pouches, a strand of gold around the middle.

"Ah." Tante smiled. "You see the little sacks they make? One morning you will wake and from the sacks will come jewels. Like magic. You will see."

Brother peered into the cage. "Wowsers."

My father started for the car. I pursued him. "Daddy, please take me with you. I miss Momma so much."

He held me by the elbows. "Listen to me, Audrey Ina. I might not mind fibbing about your age, but right now your momma can't have any company but me. I know it's hard, but you're going to have to be patient a little longer."

"And what if I can't?"

He stepped around me. "I have faith in you."

I pulled on his belt. "I won't say a word. I'll just sit and look at her."

"Oh, I believe that." He removed my hand. "Want me to give her a message?"

"Why can't I do it in person?"

"Audrey, you're not listening. I said no."

The slam of the car door sounded so final, I kicked at it with my sneaker, making a flat-sounding *thump* on the metal. My father's brow dipped. "I think you better just calm yourself down."

"I don't have to," I sassed back.

He started the engine. "I couldn't convince anyone you were twelve, the way you're acting now."

He backed the car down the driveway. I walked alongside it. "Come on, Daddy, please!" I grabbed the door handle.

The brakes squealed; the car jerked to a stop. "Step away from the car," my father commanded.

I stomped my foot. "No!"

"Audrey Ina, not everything is in my control. You should know that by now."

I put my hands to my face and sobbed in frustration. Daddy sat staring out the windshield. After a time he leaned his head out. "Want me to tell her anything or not?"

I looked away. "Fine," he said and drove off.

The car was halfway up the road when I tore after it. "Tell her I love her!" I cried.

My words went unheard. I flung myself to the ground. Next thing I knew, I had scrambled up and was running pell-mell toward the toolshed—straight for my bike.

I jumped on. Tante and Brother were bent over the cage, their backs to me. Pedaling silently, I bumped over the curb and onto the road.

It felt good being on my bike again. The air raised the hair on my arms and cooled my cheeks as I raced up Langhorne Road. Momma lay some six miles away on Route 503 going west.

I turned onto Fifth Street. American flags decorated the storefronts in readiness for tomorrow's parade. One street over, the houses were ramshackle; chickens pecked through patches of squash vines and staked tomatoes. Hardly any had cars out front.

I cut through a white neighborhood where the houses were small, the yards cluttered behind boxy hedges. Suddenly, down the street, I spied Buster LaCoste sprawled in the grass. He saw me coming and sprang into the road.

I swerved past. He grabbed his bike. My nerves jump-started. The chase was on.

Cutting north, I ducked behind the Merita Bread factory, knocking over what cans and barrels I could to roll in Buster's way. I had the lead, but he was bigger than me, and stronger.

I wound through back roads, hoping to lose him. Coming out on a crossroads, I realized I had no idea where I was. To my right stood the paper mills, hung with smoke. I backtracked toward them, fumes of paper mash stinging my nose.

Figuring I'd be safer in town, I took the shortcut back. I thought for sure I'd shaken Buster, only to have him head me off where Main Street meets Church. So I sped over to Campbell Avenue, praying there'd be traffic to lose myself among. But it was not yet ten o'clock, and church was still on.

Buster was close on my tail now. Veering off behind the Methodist church, I crashed through a patch of woods. I could hear him behind me, bumping over rocks and logs. At the edge of the woods, I turned onto a dirt road. Twisting around a curve, I skidded on gravel into a sharp piece of car fender.

Bam! My back tire popped, flipping the bike, sending me over the handlebars into a ditch. I rolled into the fall, came up bruised, and started running. Over my shoulder I saw Buster blur into view.

I'm a goner, I thought, *time to say my prayers.* And beyond the rise came a chorus of angel voices, as if to agree. The music pulled me up the hill. A tiny clapboard building sat on the riverbank below. The African Tabernacle Church of Blue Gap rang with gospel song.

The door was let open to allow in the breeze. Buster topped the hill as I flew down it, fast as my legs could carry me.

"It appears we have company." Reverend Hutcherson said from the front of the church. Heads turned to where I stood, scraped and breathless.

Frances stood. "Lord have mercy, it's Audrey Ina."

"Someone's chasing me," I managed to get out.

Mr. Cardwell got up, Sam right behind him. Other men and boys of the congregation rose also and followed them out the door. They stood before the church, watching Buster with solemn faces. He rode in circles, his face crumpled like he was crying. Finally he went up the hill, his tracks blowing into dust.

The men filed back in. I leaned against the wall, Frances beside me. "He's gone, Audrey," she said. "You're safe now."

"I couldn't think what else to do," I told her.

"You did right." She turned to the assembled. "This here's Nathan Stern's child, Audrey Ina."

Reverend Hutcherson came down the aisle. "Sorry to barge in like this, Reverend," I began.

He rocked back on his heels, laughing. "You are welcome in our church, Audrey Ina. Any daughter of Nathan Stern's is a daughter of ours." His eyes were soft. "How is your mother?"

"She's still ailing, sir."

"She's in our prayers, you tell her that."

"Yes, sir. We're enjoying the yams."

He rocked back again. I looked around at the simple

building and the curious faces. "I heard y'all singing," I declared. "I thought I'd died and gone to heaven."

"You have, child!" a woman called out. Laughter rippled through the room.

Frances took out her hanky and spit on it, wiping my face and arms. "Anything hurt you inside?"

I shook my head. "I'm real thirsty though."

"I'm gone!" Sam yelled, and ran to a spring outside, returning with a cup brimful of cool water.

Frances steered me to a wooden bench. "You sit here. We'll bring you home after."

The reverend stood at the front of the room and lifted his hands. "Lord, I take this child's presence in our midst as a sign."

Cries of "Yes, indeed!" filled the room. Paper fans beat the air like wings.

"As a fine, good omen." He stretched the words from here to next week. "That we will prevail in our struggle to be free. Lord, we beseech you to enter the heart of one Elmo Monroe and guide him to do the just thing. In Jesus' name, we pray—"

"A-men," chorused the congregation.

The reverend said, "We are going to take up collection now for Brother Cardwell's new tires. Brothers and sisters, open your hearts. And your pockets."

Pennies, nickels, dimes, and quarters found their way into the hat being passed. Somebody poked my shoulder. I turned to face a tall, grand woman, sporting a hat that bobbled with buttons and braids.

"Put your eyeballs back in your head," Frances buzzed in my ear.

"You got some bright hair, honey. Does it glow in the dark?" the woman asked, chuckling softly at her joke.

"No, ma'am," I answered, politelike.

"Where'd you get that hair anyhow?"

"From my aunt's side of the family."

"Oo-ee, it's bright," she repeated. "I like it."

"I like it, too," I said.

When the hat had made its rounds, the reverend presented its contents to Sam's daddy. "It's not much, Brother Cardwell, but it comes from the heart. We are behind you with all our soul and all our might."

Mr. Cardwell held up the hat. "This money will help pay Mr. Stern back for our new tires. We thank you. God bless you."

A woman began to sing. The others joined in, their voices swelling and carrying me with them on a tide of joy.

> Nobody knows the trouble I've seen
> Nobody knows but Jesus
> Nobody knows the trouble I've seen
> Glory hallelujah!

When the last notes had drifted off, the reverend said, "As y'all well know, the bus boycott in Montgomery is now in its sixth month."

He acknowledged shouts of "yes!" with a smile. "And it has done its work faithfully," he went on. "For I have just learned that three judges in Alabama—three *white* judges, brothers and sisters—have ruled that the bus segregation laws in that state are unconstitutional! They go against the law of the land!"

Shouts of jubilation filled the air. I could feel the

excitement on my skin. The reverend let the emotion build. "Our voices have been heard!" he cried. "The death knell for segregation has been rung!"

Thunder joined the clamor as Frances and Sam began stomping their feet. Mine added to theirs, and others too.

The reverend put up his hands to quiet us. "But the struggle is not over. Now it must be decided by the Supreme Court."

The church hummed. He dropped his voice. "There is still work to be done. The Montgomery boycott will go on. For six more months. Or six more years. Whatever it takes."

He paused to let that sink in. "Brothers and sisters, in all this time, the boycott has been carried out in a peaceful fashion. Not one Negro has spoken a harsh word or raised a hand against a white."

"Tell it!" a woman shouted.

His voice lifted. "I remind you of this, what with our Fourth of July parade upon us tomorrow. I know most of you are planning to attend. Some of you will be marching in it."

Sam grinned, nudging me. The reverend said, "Let those who are marching now rise."

Sam got to his feet; other young boys and girls rose too. "You who are marching tomorrow carry a weighty responsibility," the reverend told them. "Can we rely on you to remember the teachings of nonviolence?"

"Yes, sir!" they chorused.

"If you are personally threatened, will you be able to turn the other cheek?"

"Yes, sir!"

"And can you look with compassion upon those who would do you harm?"

"Yes, sir!"

The reverend's eyes were radiant. "I believe you. God bless you. You may sit down."

Sam sat, cheeks wet. Frances reached across me and squeezed his arm. Reverend Hutcherson brought his hands together. "Let us pray."

He bowed his head. "Lord, we ask that there be no violence tomorrow. We have friends in Blue Gap. We have enemies too. We ask for the strength to meet our battles peacefully. In Jesus' name—"

"Amen." The congregation burst into song.

> I am going to a city
> Where the roses never fade
> Here they bloom
> But for a season
> Soon their beauty is decayed
> I am going to a city
> Where the roses never fade

Listening to their voices, it seemed to me that these folks kept in their hearts the true image of a perfect world. And it made me wonder if maybe Daddy wasn't right, after all. Maybe the world *could* be changed.

18

Edwina Clark did not get her wish; the Fourth of July parade was not canceled. The day dawned hot and clear, and you could almost hear the sounds of balloons expanding and instruments being tuned, carried on the breeze. Even the stink of the mills seemed to lift, like the spirits of the town.

I lay in bed, covers over my head. I hadn't spoken to my daddy yet, but it didn't make a whit of difference. I knew full well I wasn't going anywhere today. Or ever again, for that matter.

From under the bedclothes I heard him call, "Rise and shine, Audrey Ina."

I peered out. He stood in the doorway. "Time's a-wasting," he said. "Parade won't wait for slugabeds."

I threw off the covers. "Really?"

He nodded. "Let's go. Uncle Lewis'll be here soon."

"But Daddy? Do you think it's safe?"

He smiled. "Don't fret, Tante's got that covered." My father was in a better mood this morning, and I for one was not about to question it.

Now a pipsqueak clown in a polka-dot suit burst into the room. "Ta-da!" He wore a tasseled hat over a white-powdered face.

"Who in the world is that?" I asked.

"Ha! Fooled you!" Joel pranced. "It's me, Audie!"

"Well, I'll be, Brother, look at you."

"Tante done it," he said. "I'm going to the parade."

"She made us all costumes," my daddy informed me. "Even your old fuddy-duddy father. It was her idea. She worked through the night. So as long as we're careful, we don't have to worry about being recognized, any of us."

"And is she going too?" I asked.

"Uh-huh."

"Really." The surprises were piling up. "And you're not mad at me, Daddy?"

My father turned to Joel. "Go tell Tante Audrey's up."

Brother snickered. "Audie's in trouble."

"Son."

"Bye-bye." Joel dashed from the room.

Daddy sat beside me. "I'm upset with you, Audrey Ina, don't kid yourself. You're so pigheaded sometimes, you don't listen. But maybe I wasn't listening either. It must be awful not being able to see your momma."

Reaching into his shirt pocket, he pulled out a fold of paper. "She wrote you a note."

I opened it. "This isn't her handwriting."

"She dictated it to a nurse," he explained. "Go on, read it."

Dearest Audrey,

I miss you very much. Every day I feel a little bit better, and it won't be long before I'm well enough for you to come see me.

Honey, you won't believe how many flowers and well wishes I've received. My room looks like a greenhouse! And I've got to say I'm surprised by some of the people who've sent them. If my situation can make one person see how senseless all this hatred is, maybe I can take some comfort in that.

Audrey, I know how difficult this must be for you and Joel. But you are such a strong, resilient girl, and I have so much faith in you, that I know we will all come through it just fine.

Be good to yourself. I think about you all the time.
Love,
Momma
P.S. Please water my azaleas.
P.P.S. Try not to give your daddy too hard a time. He feels bad enough as it is.

The words blurred. I looked at my father; there were tears in his eyes too. "Run get your costume on," he said.

I flew down the stairs. In the laundry room I was met by a mysterious woman turning in a swirl of cobalt blue. Swaths of silk covered her head and fell to the floor. Behind a veil, her eyes glimmered mother-of-pearl.

"Ooh, Tante," I cried. "Don't you look beautiful."

"You are saying this because it is true." She lifted her arms, the fabric rippling like water. "No one will know me in this, will they?"

"I hardly do myself."

She shifted her eyes. "There is yours. Try it on." My spacesuit hung on a hook by the washing machine.

My aunt had outdone herself. The front was crisscrossed with silver braid and there were tiny white stars appliqued on the shoulder. White piping trimmed the cuffs and set off the high collar.

"June is going to be pea green with envy," I declared, admiring myself in the mirror.

The parade was due to start at noon. At approximately eleven thirty, five strangers boarded the bus at Westerly and Langhorne. Two were dressed as *banditos*, one so round as to look suspiciously padded, a fake handlebar mustache sticking out under the brim of a sombrero. Behind the two bandits, a clown clung to the hand of a gypsy woman who floated onto the bus wearing the summer sky.

The fifth stranger had obviously just landed on Earth for the express purpose of going to the parade. She wore a helmet which, if you looked closely, was actually one of those metal colanders for draining spaghetti. She had turned it upside down and coated it with silver glitter; its legs zigzagged like antennae.

The five took their seats among monsters, hoboes, and heroes. Jack and the Giant shared a Coca-Cola, the beanstalk under their feet, while Supergirl and Dracula compared capes.

There was too much heat and hubbub to do anything but stare at the odd collection of riders. Still I couldn't help notice that the bus was less crowded than in years before.

We all got off on Church Street, since no traffic was allowed on Main the morning of the Fourth. "Stay together," Daddy cautioned.

Usually we stood in front of the library to watch the

goings-on. Only this year my father thought it wiser for us to view the parade from the safety of Uncle Lewis's second-story office.

As we turned the corner, we were greeted by Rabbi Grody, dressed in a gaily striped bathrobe, his version of Joseph's coat of many colors. On both sides of the street, floats were lined up on flatbed trucks, ready to go. Balloons flounced from parking meters, mailboxes, and rooftops. Above us, folks leaned out of upper windows, bags of confetti in hand.

A stream of people moved against the flow of foot traffic. Spying June stumbling past in a ratty fox stole and too-high heels, I called after her. She turned. "Audrey?"

"Shhh," I whispered. "I don't want to be recognized."

My friend giggled. "I wouldn't worry about it."

I grinned. "Thanks, I love you too. Only where you going? The parade's thataway." I pointed in the direction of the library.

"Oh, I'm so mad I could spit," June declared. "We have to leave."

"Why?"

She lowered her voice. "Guess you ain't gotten a load of Miss Farley yet."

"Uh-oh. What's that woman up to?"

June shook her head. "Mommy didn't want to come at all and now she's acting like the sky is going to fall."

Her eyes darted to someone behind me; I knew without turning it was my father. "June," I said, "I'll call and tell you all about the parade." Falling in behind Daddy, I yelled back, "Who you got up as anyway?"

"A famous actress," she replied.

"Which one?"

She dropped her voice. "June Silverman, darling." And tossing the stole over her shoulder, she tripped after her mother and the departing crowd.

In front of Uncle Lewis's building, the librarian's voice rose above the tumult. "Daddy?" I asked. "Can we go visit Miss Farley? I promised I would."

"After the parade." He gestured impatiently. "Come on, it's near twelve."

As Uncle Lewis unlocked the front door, I glanced the other way down Main. Edwina and her mother were standing beside the float for the Daughters of the American Revolution. They wore long handmade dresses and moppy little caps; Mrs. Clark was holding a mirror so her daughter could primp.

I said, "Daddy, there's someone I've got to see."

"Not now, Audrey."

The others were headed up the stairs. "One minute, that's all I ask. Please. It's important."

"It better be. You have sixty seconds, young lady. Get going."

My feet carried me through the crowd. Closer to Edwina, I saw that her hem dragged the ground. Coming up behind her as quietly as I could, I dug my heel into it.

Then borrowing June's actressy tone, I whispered, "Excuse me, but there's an enormous black spider crawling up your—"

Before I could even finish, Edwina had screamed and fled. There was a quick tearing sound and I looked down to find the back of her dress from waist to hem laying under my foot. As I turned away, I caught a glimpse of

Mrs. Clark's face, watching her daughter run down the street, underpants showing.

"—fifty-eight, fifty-nine—" my father was saying as I ran back. "What was all that squawking about?" I started up the stairs without answering.

"Audrey Ina."

I didn't look around. "Daddy, I can't help it if our costumes are better made than most."

Tante stood at the window of my uncle's office. She turned as I came in. "Do you see this?" she asked in wonder.

I peered over the crowd. There was Miss Farley, resplendent in her gown, holding up her torch, crown askew. Behind her was a larger-than-life copy of the Declaration of Independence, with the familiar curlicues and bold signatures below.

Mr. Monroe stood nearby, arms crossed, his eye on the folks gathered before the librarian. "On this Fourth of July," she was intoning, "in the year nineteen hundred fifty-six—one hundred eighty years after the original Fourth—I declare the Blue Gap Public Library integrated."

Boos greeted her announcement. "Can she decide that, Daddy?" I breathed. "All by herself?"

"Looks like she has, doesn't it?" he replied.

The courthouse clock began to chime the noon hour; the crowd made its way to the curb. Miss Farley kept on till the opening band struck up a lively version of "God Bless America" and drowned her out. The long-awaited Fourth of July parade had officially begun.

Jugglers and acrobats burst onto the street. Uncle

Lewis passed out paper sacks of confetti and we rained down showers on proud veterans from both world wars. They marched behind an old-timer from the Spanish-American War, a shrunken man in a rickety wheelchair.

The Shriners followed, in their bright red fezzes. Then came the clowns, wriggling between papier-mâchè elephants and stilted giraffes. Majorettes high-stepped before the white high school band, batons twirling. Cheers crescendoed as the floats charmed the happy crowd.

The Daughters of the American Revolution rode by, identical Betsy Rosses sewing on an old-timey flag. Edwina sat with the flag in folds across her lap, furious blotches dotting each cheek.

Joel perched in Daddy's arms, shouting as each new marvel came into view. In some ways this year's parade was no different from any other year, a noisy, cheerful march of Blue Gap citizens.

At last the Dunbar band marched by, its junior and varsity football teams in straight rows behind. The crowd watched them pass with uneasy curiosity. I searched the ranks for Sam. Here he came, grinning under the dome of his helmet. Daddy pointed him out to Joel. "Yay, Sam!" Brother cried.

All at once something hit Sam's shoulder, splattering yellow and giving off a horrid smell. Another small explosion left a red gush on the boy beside him. More followed in quick succession: *plop! plop! plop!* The team was being pelted with tomatoes and rotten eggs.

The music broke off. In the confusion I heard the reverend yell, "Play! Keep playing!" The band started up again and the marchers stayed in step, even as their uniforms were pummeled yellow and red.

From our window we could see where the troublemakers were standing. There were several of them, boys mostly, blocked from the crowd by a stand of maples.

My father leaned from the window. "Elmo!" he shouted, waving his arms. "There they are!" His sombrero slipped from his head. He grabbed for it but it plunged to the street below.

"There's Stern!" someone shouted, and almost immediately a tomato smashed above Daddy's head.

"Get down!" he yelled. We backed away from the window. Uncle Lewis slammed it shut. An egg hit the glass, running yellow goo.

Keeping low, I snuck back to the sill. Mr. Monroe had routed the attackers; their scattering jostled folks into the street. Buster tore around to the library and wasted no time in dragging Miss Farley's Declaration to the ground. She gave an awful shriek and batted him with her torch.

He dashed off, the librarian in pursuit, holding her muddied skirts. "Stop that boy!"

The police chief made his way through the crush. Buster snaked into the crowd, pushing folks this way and that, till he rounded the corner and could be seen no more.

My father turned to Uncle Lewis. "I don't think we should stay now that I've been recognized."

"I was thinking the same thing," my uncle replied.

His waiting room windows looked out on a back alley. From them we could see swarms of people scurrying away from the commotion.

My father said, "We'll split up. Lewis, you get Tante and the kids home."

"Daddy, no," I protested.

"Audrey, it's safer for everybody if I take my own chances."

"You can't go by yourself," I insisted. "It's too dangerous—"

"She is right, Nathan," Tante cut in. "You should not be alone. Lewis can go with you. I will get the children home."

My father held her look. "All right. Wait a few minutes, then take them out the back way."

"Here, Nat." Uncle Lewis handed Daddy his Stetson and the two brothers went out the door.

"Be careful," I called, watching from the window as they slipped down a side alley.

Tante knelt beside Joel. "I will put you on my back. Do not let go, no matter what."

Below us, the crowd was still scrambling in confusion. After a minute my aunt held out her hand to me. "Come."

The three of us flew down the stairs into the alley where a surge of people swept us along. My helmet toppled into the gutter; a foot squashed it beyond repair. Cutting down a narrow side street, we came out on Church just as a bus lumbered past. "Wait!" Tante cried. It slowed and stopped.

The door opened as we ran up to it. "We don't have any money," I told the driver, panting.

"What happened?" he asked. Other folks came up behind us, also wanting to be let on.

"Some guys threw stuff at the Dunbar team," I said.

"Get in," he replied.

We rushed on, taking seats in the middle, me on the aisle and Joel in Tante's lap. Sweat poured down my face, leaving chalky streaks on my costume. "Everything's ruined," I cried. "Mr. Monroe will never hire Mr. Cardwell now."

"Audrey, please." My aunt's veil had slipped from her forehead; her face was flushed. "Let us just get home safe."

The bus followed the trail of blackened confetti and tattered streamers that marked the path of the parade. It squealed to a stop to let on more passengers, many with their costumes in shambles.

The bus was nearly full now, save for three or four empty seats down front. After a while Edwina and her mother came on, Edwina holding the back of her skirt. They sank into seats behind the driver.

Everyone was jabbering about the attack. The chatter cut off sharply when the Dunbar team got on, Sam among them. They walked to the back, uniforms stained, heads high. Taking up the remaining seats in the Negro section, their overflow filled the aisle.

Sam stood close by me. I could see him eyeing the empty seats. After all he'd been through, here was yet another humiliation. It was more than I could bear, seeing him have to stand.

Heart knocking, I got to my feet. "You look plumb worn out, Sam." I indicated my seat. "Why don't you sit down?"

A tremor went through the bus. I kept my gaze on

Sam. Our eyes met. "Don't mind if I do," he replied, and plunked down beside my aunt.

In the shocked silence, the driver glanced in his rearview mirror. Edwina jumped to her feet, shouting, "I knew it was you in that getup, Audrey Stern! I knew it, I knew it!"

The bus swerved to the curb. Sam tensed. I held my breath.

The door swung open. "If anybody's got a problem being on this bus," the driver drawled, "they can get off right now. I'll give you a transfer."

Little Bo Peep ran down the aisle, snatching a pink slip out of his hand. "Anyone else?" he demanded.

No one moved. Mrs. Clark rose. "I don't know what the world is coming to when wayward children can break the law and nobody seems to mind—"

"Oh, sit down, Mother." Edwina plopped in her seat. "As if people care what you think."

"Last call," the driver said.

"Shut up and drive," a man returned. "It's hot."

The door clanged closed and the bus rolled on. Sam and I cut our eyes at each other. A slow grin began its way across his face.

19

Sometimes big things happen in small ways. July fifth came and went in a humid haze and the only thing that marked it different from any other summer day was that Blue Gap got a Negro police officer.

The news spread like a flame on a fuse that never did explode. My daddy said that what cinched it for Mr. Monroe was the incident on the bus with Sam and me. In spite of everything, even the trouble at the parade, the fact that folks didn't object to Sam sitting in a seat up front convinced him that Blue Gap might be ready for Mr. Cardwell after all. He said it was the sign he'd been waiting for.

I wasn't so sure about that. When I thought about it afterward, seemed to me like Mr. Monroe made up his mind that afternoon in the alley when Mr. Cardwell saved Tante and me from those three racists. Of course I'd been mistaken about that man before.

The days flew by and except for the unaccustomed sight of Mr. Cardwell in the patrol car, folks appeared to go about their business pretty much as usual. I had to wonder about that too. I'd seen how hatred could fester under a polite surface, so I couldn't help worry that maybe nothing had changed.

Momma was getting stronger every day. It wouldn't be long before she was home to stay. The doctor thought she'd have some scars on her face; she might even need an operation on her leg. Plans were being made to repair the house in August, so she and Joel were going to stay at Grandma Lena's in Charlottesville where she could rest up properlike.

Miss Farley had been told to petition town council if she was serious about integrating the library. She was all set to go to the July meeting. Last we spoke, she was still trying to decide whether or not to appear in her Statue of Liberty costume.

One morning we awoke and just as Tante had predicted, there were jewels in Joel's cage. Orange-bright monarch butterflies hung from the mesh, clapping their wings behind them, as if applauding their own arrival. That evening the three of us let them go in the field behind the house. As they glided over the milkweed, I told Brother and Tante about how butterflies had once been part of a star.

July melted into August; dog days panted at the door. They showed up every summer about the time Sirius, the dog star, returned to the night sky, sparkling over the horizon in a wash of dawn. Sirius brought with it the Perseid meteor showers.

The Perseids happen when the Earth, in its orbit around the Sun, passes through what's left of a comet's tail. Big dirty snowballs, comets swing in from the far reaches of the solar system, loop around the Sun, and leave behind a trail of rubble and dust. When that trail burns up in our atmosphere, we see the Perseid shooting stars.

Usually Daddy watched them with me. Only this August he was away visiting Momma and Brother at Grandma's. So one fine night Tante joined me in the yard. A breeze played over the grass; katydids chirred their treetop fandango.

The show began after midnight. We sat under the sweet gum oohing and aahing at the fiery bursts of yellow, orange, green, and red streaking across the sky, sometimes three or four at a time, with long sizzling tails.

"Oh, Tante," I marveled, after an especially thrilling display. "Isn't it just like having a seat at the beginning of time? Imagine stars and planets being born before our very eyes."

"You are making me feel quite old," she answered.

I smiled. "You ever wonder what might happen if the Earth was made all over again? From scratch, I mean. Do you suppose we'd turn out any different?"

Her eyes mirrored the sky. "It would be nice to think so."

A meteor sailed above us, its tail a spray of glittering sparks. It put me in mind of the shattered glass from the broken window at Daddy's factory, and the Shabbos night two months ago when the whole summer began.

"Tante—?" I hesitated. "Do you believe in God?"

My question hung in the air. After a time she raised a hand to the sky. "What do you call this?" she asked.

"That's the Big Dipper," I told her.

"Ah. In my country we call this *Woz Niebeski*."

"Woz Niebeski." I stumbled over the Polish sounds. "What does it mean?"

"How do you say—? Wagon of Heaven." Her smile was sad. "In Jarzyna I imagine God pulling this wagon. And I would think of all the things He carried in it. Fire to make the stars, dust for planets. But in Auschwitz, even the stars betray me. I cannot believe they still dare to shine."

Her voice trembled. "You cannot know what it is to lose everyone you love and have nothing of them. Not a grave, a thimble, nothing."

I took a deep breath. "But—there's the photograph."

"What photograph?"

"Of your family, don't you remember? My mother told you about it."

"A photograph," she echoed, memory jogged.

I bolted into the house, up to my room, flying back with the fold of tissue paper in my hand. I placed it on her lap. "Here, Tante. This belongs to you."

"What is this?" She hid her face. "I do not want this. Take it away."

I waited. When she uncovered her eyes, I turned on the flashlight so she could see. She pulled the paper apart with trembling fingers. "Dear God," she murmured as her family came into view.

She could not bring herself to touch it, but merely gazed at the faces. After a while she held the photo up to her cheek. A cry rose from inside her and flung itself against the night. I thought for sure the stars must hear her, so long and hard did she cry.

By the time her tears were spent, the Perseids had faded. Sirius rose in the east, a flickering jewel. Tante regarded me a long moment.

"What is it?" I asked.

She shook her head. "Strange thoughts come into my mind. I am thinking, maybe when I come to Virginia, I do not know I have a sister waiting here for me."

We looked at each other and looked away; shyness settled over us. In the silver sky, Sirius floated on crimson clouds.

"Tante—" I stopped. "I don't know, what should I call you now?"

She thought a moment. "For two years I have no name. Then I come here and I find I am this Tante. Please. I think I am longing for you to call me Pesel."

She leaned over and brushed my cheek with her lips. "Good night, Audrey Ina."

I slid my arms around her. "Sweet dreams, Pesel."

The kitchen door closed behind her. Soon the light in her room came on. I was in the yard when it went out again.

I gazed up. I still believed there were beings out in space, waiting to get to know us. But now I knew why they hadn't gotten in touch yet. We weren't ready. We had to learn to get along with each other first.

The world was full of brutal things, worse than you could ever imagine. But at the same time, it was filled with amazing things. Like shooting stars and butterflies being born and learning how to love. It was a paradox.

The universe wheeled above me, an endless mystery. And suddenly my mind stretched into the galaxy and my heart danced among the stars. I was fire and air and emptiness, burning and changing. I was water and soil and flowers. I was people too, with all their joys and sorrows. I was everything at once.

Then the feeling faded and I was just a girl sitting in a backyard. The wind stirred against my cheek, carrying autumn on it. Soon school would be starting up again. It was hard to believe so much had happened in so short a time. Dr. Einstein was right. You could live a whole lifetime in a second sometimes, when you traveled at the speed of light.